TAXES AND TARDIS

N.R. WALKER

BLURB

Brent is a jock, Logan a geek; these men are a world apart. But if opposites attract, maybe it's the differences between them that make it worth the fight.

Brent Kelly is a laid-back electrician whose only concerns are drinks with friends and which man to bed next. In need of a new accountant to sort out his nightmarish shoebox of tax receipts, he's referred to Logan Willis.

He doesn't expect to be intrigued by the science fiction-loving, geeky guy with dark-rimmed glasses and a TARDIS-blue shirt. So his fascination with the soft-spoken Englishman surprises him, and their mutual attraction is completely unexpected. He most certainly never expects to fall in love.

One a jock and the other a geek, both men know the differences between them are vast and could cause problems. But in this opposites-attract erotic drama, maybe it's the differences between them that make staying together worth the fight.

COPYRIGHT

Star Wars: Lucasfilm

The X-Files: Fox

Treasure Island: Robert Louis Stevenson

Any and all *Star Wars* references: Lucasfilm;

Any and all *Star Trek* references: Gene Roddenberry, CBS and Paramount Pictures

Taxes *and* TARDIS

N.R. Walker

CHAPTER ONE

TRAFFIC ON A FRIDAY afternoon in the central business district was hell. After two laps around the block, I finally found a parking space. I pulled my truck into the too-damned-small spot, grabbed the old shoebox off the front seat, and walked quickly back to my intended destination.

It wasn't very often I ventured into the business district. And as I walked into the building fronted by glass, I remembered why. My reflection was a stark reminder of just how underdressed I was. Compared to the expensive suits walking around filled with their own importance, my work boots and plaid overshirt were somewhat outclassed.

Following the signs, I walked down the expensive hall to the expensive office with the expensive desk. "Brent Kelly," I said, introducing myself to the receptionist. "I have a three o'clock appointment." I looked at my watch. "Which I'm a little late for."

I smiled apologetically at her, hoping my scruffy blond hair, dark blue eyes, and three-day growth would come off as rugged charm. I knew my looks could work in my favor with most women. Not my usual intended target, but hey, whatever worked.

She looked at me, my clothes, and the box in my hand, and she smiled. "Take a seat, Mr. Kelly," she offered kindly. "Logan will be with you shortly."

Logan. My new accountant.

I hadn't believed it when I'd called my old accountant to make my annual tax appointment and was told she'd been taken ill. All her clients were being referred to new accountants downtown. Well, they weren't new; they were just new to me. They were quite old and reputable, and I could just picture this Logan as a bean-counting dinosaur.

My accounts were a shamble. I knew that, and so did my old accountant. I'd gone to her for years. I'd hand over my shoebox of receipts and tax invoices with a warm smile, and she'd just do it all for me. Now I'd have to start from scratch, explaining everything to this new guy.

I was going to be there for hours.

"Mr. Kelly?" I looked up to see the receptionist now standing in front of me. "Logan will see you now," she said with a professional smile. She walked toward the open door at the other end of the room, and I presumed I was to follow.

She led me down the dark mahogany hall, and about halfway down the corridor, she showed me into a dark office with a wall of books where a guy sat behind the desk, scribbling in a file. With another professional smile and not another word, the receptionist turned and left, and there I was standing in front of a desk and a guy who still hadn't even looked up.

I cleared my throat nervously. "Um…"

Only then did he look at me. "Yes, Mr. Kelly, please take a seat."

I noticed his English accent first. Then the fact that he

wasn't old like I'd presumed he would be. In fact, he didn't look any older than me, maybe twenty-four, twenty-five. He had short, dark brown hair, pink lips, and blue-gray eyes behind dark-rimmed glasses.

He looked at me for half a second, blinked, then looked back down at his paperwork. Typical pen-pusher. Typical bean-counter.

Nerd.

Geek.

I rolled my eyes in frustration, took a seat across from him, and put my shoebox on the seat next to me. "Sorry I was late. I got held up at work, then traffic into the city was bad. Took forever to find a parking space."

He looked up from his desk at me. "That's okay." Then he cleared his throat and shook his head. "I've been going through your files sent over from your previous accountant," he said casually, pushing his glasses up on the bridge of his nose. "I thought the shoebox might have been an exaggeration." He smiled, as though he found me amusing.

I sighed. "Uh… no. It's been my filing system for years…"

"Yes, that's what it says here," he said, tapping the file in front of him.

"Oh." I couldn't help being a bit embarrassed. "Yeah, um… Accounts are not my forte."

He pulled out a clean piece of paper, pushed his glasses back up on his nose, and looked at me. "So, Mr. Kelly," he started.

"Please, call me Brent."

"Okay, Brent, I'll need some background information."

So I started at the beginning. I told him I was an electrician by trade, self-employed, and subcontracted to one of the biggest construction companies in San Antonio.

He asked questions about pension, taxes, and insurance. He pulled my shoebox over and started leafing through the mess inside while he talked about income, expenses, deductibles, and whatever else, stopping every now and then only to push his glasses up on his nose.

His accent made everything he said sound musical and soft, which was a weird thing for me to notice. As was the color of his shirt. It was a normal long-sleeved business shirt, but it was the bluest blue I thought I'd ever seen. He wore a darker blue tie and had a black vest on over the top.

I watched his fingers—his long, slender fingers—as he tapped them lightly on the page in front of him, and how he held the pen, and I watched his lips as he spoke. He had pink, even lips, and his pale British skin was like cream. He really wasn't my type at all. I'd never been one for the studious kind. I preferred the athletic, adventurous type, but I found myself staring at him.

I didn't know why I couldn't stop staring as he spoke, the way his lips moved, his accent—God, his accent—how the too-blue shirt looked against his slender, pale neck; how the shirt highlighted the flecks of blue in his eyes; how his glasses didn't make him look geeky, just smarter, cuter. I stared at him as he talked numbers, wondering... daydreaming... fantasizing about what he smelled like, what he tasted like...

"Brent?"

My name snapped my attention back to what he was saying, rather than where my mind had just gone. I shook my head. "Yeah?"

"I asked if you'd categorized your tax holdings?"

"I'm sorry." I shrugged. "You lost me at pension."

He smiled and put down his pen. He really did have a pretty smile. "It's obvious you're not interested—"

"Yes, I am," I said too quickly, interrupting him. Interested? In him? Oh, hell…

He blinked, seemingly surprised by my quick response. "Interested in your accounts?"

"Um, I try to be," I said with a shrug, looking around the room. "It's just that I'm not very good at it."

"Hmm," he hummed with a thoughtful nod. "This will take some time," he murmured, though I think it was more to himself than to me. His long, delicate fingers rubbed over the smooth skin of his jaw. "I guess I could work on it over the weekend."

"I don't want to be a bother," I told him honestly. One eyebrow lifted behind the dark rim of his glasses, as though he didn't believe me. "If there's anything I can do…" I stopped talking when I realized how stupid I sounded. "Well…" I cleared my throat. "If there's anything I can do besides being better at my accounts."

He looked at me and grinned. I think he almost laughed.

I nodded with a chuckle. "Yeah, I'm really not very good at anything with numbers."

He chuckled that time and looked pointedly at the shoebox of receipts. "I can see that."

I smiled at him and nodded, and in that moment of silence when I shouldn't have said anything, I opened my mouth. "Your shirt is really blue."

He blinked, taken aback by my not-related-to-accounts comment. "Oh," he mumbled, a little embarrassed. "It was a birthday gift from my sister."

"It's very blue. Is it like a peacock blue?" God, why couldn't I just shut up?

"Um, no." He shifted in his seat. "It's TARDIS blue."

TARDIS… TARDIS… What the hell was a TARDIS? "TARDIS?"

He swallowed loudly. "Time and Relative Dimension in Space," he said quietly. "The telephone box from *Doctor Who*."

"Really?" I snorted. Was he kidding? Oh my God, no, he really wasn't.

He stared at me, unmoving, and mumbled, "Yes. I happen to like *Doctor Who*."

Oh, fuck. "Sure," I amended quickly. "I'm sure it's great. It's just that I'm not that familiar with it, that's all." I groaned inwardly. Talk about awkward. I changed the subject. "So about these accounts…"

He pushed his glasses back up on his nose. "I'll have a look over them this weekend," he told me.

"Um, I don't want to interrupt your plans." Then, because my brain-to-mouth filter was on vacation, I said, "If your girlfriend doesn't mind." His eyes widened as the stupidity poured out of my mouth, so I tried to fix it. "Or your boyfriend. I mean, I don't want you to think you have to do it this weekend. I'm sure I can take my box of stuff and sort it, at least…"

His mouth fell open in shock, and he blinked. Twice.

"Oh, Jesus," I mumbled, horrified. "Sorry."

He blinked again.

I closed my eyes, wishing that my stupidity would just disappear. "Sorry. I didn't… I mean…" I groaned, and taking a deep breath, I started again. "How about I take this," I said, reaching out and picking up my old shoebox off the desk, "and give the office a call when I have them sorted?"

I stood up, mortified at my inability to think or speak in front of this guy, and walked to the door.

"Brent?"

I turned around, thinking he'd tell me he'd hand my files over to another accountant. He surprised me by walking around the desk toward me. And there we stood, facing each other, him in his expensive suit pants and vest and me in my dirty work clothes and boots, with my stupid mouth. He reached out and took the shoebox from me. "I'll take these," he said, clearly amused.

I wasn't expecting him to be as tall as me. His height surprised me, and as I opened my mouth to say something, only more stupid came out. "You're tall."

He laughed at me, and I wished the ground would open up and swallow me whole. But then I was suddenly aware of how close he was, and how he matched my six-foot height, how his eyes were in direct line with mine. He was still smiling. "Do you always struggle in social situations?"

I looked into his blue-gray eyes and shook my head slowly. "Not normally, no."

He stared at me, tilting his head to the side. "And to answer your assumption from before, no, I don't have a boyfriend."

"Neither do I," I blurted out. Then I let out an embarrassed huff and tried to talk some sense. "Have a boyfriend, that is. I mean, yes, I'm gay, but I'm not seeing anyone."

And he smiled at me. Not an I'm-glad-you're-single kind of smile, but more of an I'm-smiling-because-you're-an-idiot kind of smile. I shook my head. Me, Brent Kelly, who played football, who could pick up any guy with just a suggestive nod, was being bent all out of shape by a bean-counting nerd.

A tall, delicate, bean-counting nerd. A totally cute, funny, really smart, British, bean-counting nerd with pink lips and long fingers. And a TARDIS-colored shirt.

Still smiling, he walked back to his desk. "I have your details if I need anything else," he told me. But then he put down the shoebox and picked up a business card. "This is me," he said, handing me the small slip of cardboard. He pushed his glasses back up on his nose. "If you need to contact me, you can phone my cell after hours."

And just like that, he very smoothly gave me his number. I took the card and read his name. "Well, Logan Willis, CPA, I might just do that."

The corner of his mouth almost lifted in a smile, but he tilted his head as though he was trying to figure something out. His eyes were intense behind his glasses, like he was trying to find the answers on my face.

I stared back at him, wondering what he was looking for, and I wondered what he found when he huffed quietly and shook his head. "Okay, then," he said with a puzzled smile.

"Okay, then," I repeated with a nod.

I left him with the shoebox of receipts and papers, took his phone number with me, and went home on a mission. I really needed to ease the ache in my dick. And I really, *really* needed to find out what the fuck a TARDIS was.

CHAPTER TWO

I PULLED my truck into my parking spot in front of my place, took the DVDs off the front seat, and went inside. Tim's truck was parked in the drive. I was surprised he was still home.

"Hey," Tim greeted me with smiling brown eyes and his freshly showered, scraggly blond hair. "I was wonderin' where you were."

"Hey," I returned his greeting. "Thought you'd be out already."

"Got home late." He looked at me still dressed in work clothes. "You comin' or not?"

"Ah, no," I hedged. "I might have a night in."

Tim blinked and stared at me like I'd just sprouted a second head.

We'd known each other since we'd both been apprentices and had moved in together when we'd turned eighteen. We were very similar—both electricians, both single, both liked to go out for a drink on weekends. We'd both pick up one-night stands, only he brought women home and I brought men. He didn't care that I was gay. He was laid-back, easy to get along with, easy to live with. He was my best friend.

He still looked confused. "You're not coming?"

I looked down at the videos I was holding. "Um…"

"What the hell is that?" he asked, even more confused. "Are those porn videos?"

"Um, no…" I held the DVDs up so he could see the covers.

He looked at the DVDs, then looked at me, wide-eyed. "You seriously aren't coming out with me and the guys so you can spend Friday night watching *Doctor Who*?"

"Um…"

He rolled his eyes and shook his head. "Did you sniff the industrial adhesive at work today?"

I laughed, pulled off my overshirt, kicked my boots off, then grabbed a beer from the fridge. I slid the first disc into the DVD player just as Tim called out, "Last chance."

"Nah," I replied, falling onto the sofa. "I'm good. You go. Tell the guys I said hi."

He snorted. "Well, I'm certainly not gonna tell them you're watching *Doctor* friggin' *Who*, that's for sure. Marty will be around in a flash to give you mouth to mouth."

I rolled my eyes at him, picked up the remote, stretched my feet out on the sofa, and pressed play.

I'd searched up the address of a specialist sci-fi store, and when I'd walked in, I'd asked the young girl behind the counter where I could find anything on *Doctor Who*. She'd pointed me in the right direction, but among a whole bunch of merchandise there were so many DVDs I hadn't been really sure on where to start.

I'd picked up one, only because it had a blue, old-fashioned telephone box on the front. That had to be the TARDIS. I'd smiled. But the guy with curly hair and hokey scarf had looked too 70s, so I'd put it back. I'd found other ones, which looked more modern and were the Tenth Doctor series apparently, so I collected three of those instead.

I'd always liked science fiction. And by that, I mean I'd watched all the *Star Wars* films and most episodes of *The X-Files*. But this was rather engaging. Not saying I'd be running out to buy a TARDIS blue shirt anytime soon, but I sat through the first DVD—which had three episodes on it—and rather enjoyed it.

I put the second disc in, and as I waited for the episodes to start, I walked into the kitchen to grab something to eat. I noticed a business card on the floor, and realizing it must have fallen out of my shirt pocket when I pulled it off, I picked up the card and turned it over.

Logan Willis.

I grabbed a second beer, took the card, and sat back down in the living room just as the second disc's episodes started to play. But I really didn't watch much of the show. I stared at the small rectangle of cardboard, and before I lost my nerve, I took out my cell and dialed his number.

He answered on the second ring. "Hello?"

His British accent made me smile. "Uh, Logan? This is Brent Kelly."

There was a long pause. "Yes?"

He sounded so unsure, and I wondered if I'd done the right thing by calling. Figuring I couldn't look any more of an idiot than I had earlier, I really had nothing to lose. "So, this Doctor Who guy travels to different galaxies in the TARDIS thing?" There was only silence on the line, so as always, I felt the need to fill it. "Because it's not very aerodynamic, and it doesn't seem like it's built to withstand the pressure of zero gravity."

After another beat of silence, he said, "The TARDISes are grown, not built."

Then it was me who was silent, replaying his words over in my mind. "Huh?"

He huffed out a laugh. "Never mind. Are you watching *Doctor Who?*"

"Yeah," I admitted. "It's not bad."

He laughed again. "Which episodes?"

"Oh, I dunno," I started, but then grabbed the DVD cover. "It's the second disc of the Tenth Doctor…?" My uncertain tone made it almost a question.

"Ah," he said. "David Tennant."

"Who?"

"Never mind," he chuckled again. "Can I ask why you're watching it?"

"Um, your shirt," I admitted. "I had no idea what a TARDIS was, and you mentioned *Doctor Who*… so I figured I'd start there."

"And do you like it?" he asked. His British accent sounded just as nice on the phone.

"Well," I sighed. "I don't think I'll be camping out at the next convention, but it's not too bad."

He laughed again. I was making him laugh, and I quite liked that.

"You seem to be a little more conversational than you were earlier."

"Oh, you mean the ability to speak?" I said with a laugh. "Maybe it's because you're not in front of me, making me all flustered."

"Flustered?" he asked, incredulously. Then he snorted. "Not likely."

"Yes, likely," I told him without shame. "I might not be too good with keeping my accounts organized, but I can normally talk, yes."

He chuckled down the line, then he sighed. "So, you called me because…?"

"To ask you about the flying telephone box."

"You mean the TARDIS."

"Mm-hmm," I hummed, stretching back out on the sofa, getting comfortable. "I thought if I was going to buy three DVDs of it, I might as well get someone to explain it to me."

"You bought three DVDs of *Doctor Who?*"

"Yeah," I said, then took a mouthful of my beer. "I haven't spent a Friday night at home watching TV in ages. You saved me about fifty bucks and a hangover tomorrow."

He chuckled again. "So you're telling me I should adjust your books to allow fifty dollars per week in beverage allowance?"

"Is beer tax deductible?"

"Ah, no."

"Is buying *Doctor Who* DVDs deductible?"

"Are they educational to your profession?"

"They could be."

He laughed. "That depends on your accountant."

"Well, he's a fan," I told him. "He has a shirt that's TARDIS blue."

He laughed again, a quiet, deep, musical that made me smile.

As much as I was enjoying the banter, I changed the subject. "So what did I interrupt? What are you doing tonight?"

"Work," he answered. "Some guy dropped off a shoebox full of receipts and invoices. I'll be trying to reconcile his books for a while."

I grimaced. "Oh, that's too bad. Was he at least cute?"

There was a beat of silence before he answered. "Not too bad."

I snorted out a laugh. "Not too bad? Oh, that's rough. You should at least make him help you."

He cleared his throat nervously. "And how would he do that?"

"He could bring you lunch tomorrow, and you could both go through all that paperwork together."

"Mmm." It sounded as though he was smiling. "I don't know… he's not very good at doing accounts." And just when I thought he was going to say no, he said, "Would he bring the *Doctor Who* DVDs?"

"I'm sure he could," I answered with a smile.

"Okay," he said simply. He gave me his address and we talked for a while longer. The conversation between us just seemed so easy, nothing too personal, and nothing at all like our earlier encounter in his office. I at least held my own side of this conversation. I even made him laugh a few more times before I told him I'd see him tomorrow, and we said goodbye.

I just hoped I'd be able to actually speak when I was in front of him again.

CHAPTER THREE

I WAS UNCHARACTERISTICALLY nervous and at a loss
to explain why. This guy, Logan, was nothing like the usual
guys I pursued. My normal type of guy was similar to me
—bigger, more athletic, tanned. Sure, I'd had my share of
twinks, but Logan wasn't even a twink. He just wasn't as
masculine, as manly, as my usual type.

He was slim, lean, and delicate. His face was pale and,
dare I say it, pretty. Certainly not the sporty type or the
outdoorsy type, he was geeky, a nerd. He was an accountant who wore a vest, thick, rimmed glasses, and watched
science fiction. He couldn't be any further from my type.

So I really was at a loss as to why I was so nervous.

But I wanted him to like me. I wanted to impress him. I
wanted to make him laugh when I was with him so I could
see what he looked like when he threw his head back with
abandon.

I wondered if his skin was as soft as it looked. I
wondered if his lips were too. I wondered what he tasted
like.

I groaned. Fucking hell. I'd already rubbed one out in

the shower, and yet here I stood at the door to his apartment, and my cock twitched again at the mere thought of him.

It wasn't bad enough that it was him I'd imagined as I'd pumped myself in the shower. It was his lips against mine I'd imagined as I'd stroked my dick. It was his lips I'd imagined around me, licking and sucking as I'd pulled and swiped my fist over the head of my cock. It was his creamy white ass I'd imagined sinking deep inside of as my orgasm barreled through me, spurting cum over the tiles. My head had spun with images of him as the feeling in my legs had returned and until the water had run cold.

I wondered how on earth I'd spend the next few hours in the same room as him without getting a hard-on when just the thought of him had my dick twitching. Then he opened the door.

I almost groaned.

There he stood, all British-pale skin and dark-rimmed glasses. And he smiled. He was wearing tight black jeans, a white T-shirt, and a gray golfer's vest. Not a look many could wear, but he looked… cute.

I swallowed thickly. "Hey." I held up a bag with our lunch in one hand and the three DVDs in the other.

He stood aside in a silent invitation and I walked inside his apartment. The space was very nice, very modern and sleek, like it was fresh off the cover of *Single Gay Living*. It was all blacks and whites and grays, but it somehow still managed to be warm.

It was an open space with a black leather sofa and a dining table in front of a large window, next to a stylish kitchen. I headed in that general direction and put the DVDs on the counter along with lunch. "I, um, I didn't really know what to get for lunch, but there's this little shop near my place that does chicken souvlaki and a Greek salad…"

"Sounds great," he said softly, adjusting his glasses. And strangely enough, it was he who seemed nervous.

I suggested we eat first, while the chicken was still warm, but when I looked to the dining table, I saw it was covered in papers. On closer inspection, I realized the entire table was covered in my papers. "Oh," I mumbled. "Is that all mine?"

"I just finished putting them into categories for tax purposes," he told me.

I cringed and looked at him apologetically. "Sorry."

He smiled. "It's fine, really." He grabbed some plates and cutlery and suggested we eat in the living room, putting the plates on the coffee table. Then he took two cushions off the sofa and put them on the floor, one on either side of the coffee table, and I presumed one of them was now my seat.

Logan sat down on one cushion, easily folding his long, lean legs underneath himself. He was quiet and graceful, whereas I sat down like a lug on the other cushion facing him. I had to sit cross-legged like I had in grade school. Actually, the last time I'd sat like that *was* in grade school.

"Ugh," I groaned. "Jeez, haven't had to sit like this in a while."

"Oh," he said, alarmed. "We can sit on the sofa…"

Oh, shit. "No, no," I quickly amended. "It's fine. Just my legs don't fold up around my ears as easy as yours." He ducked his head and a pink hue tinted his cheeks as I replayed my words in my head. "Oh, um… I didn't mean… Oh, God," I mumbled. "See what I mean about flustered?"

He pushed his glasses up on his nose and smiled. "I think I'm beginning to, yes."

I let out an embarrassed laugh. "I can go into the next room and call your cell if you'd like to have a proper conversation with me."

He stared at his empty plate. "Why do I make you flustered?"

I shrugged, suddenly feeling a little awkward. "Um… because you're smart, and I'm not." His head shot up. He looked at me with wide eyes, so I explained. "The more I try not to say something stupid, the stupider I sound."

He blinked, startled. Then he opened his mouth as if to say something, but closed it again, obviously not sure how to reply. He pushed his glasses up on his nose again and started dishing up lunch. But then he said, "I'm not that smart, and you're definitely not not-smart. You're obviously good at what you do. You're self-employed. That takes some know-how."

I shrugged, a little embarrassed. "Maybe."

He gave me a small smile as he put one plate in front of me. "This looks good," he said, nodding toward his own plate. "Thanks."

Talking was easier as we ate our lunch. I told him about my roommate, Tim, how he was my best friend, how he'd come home drunk and obnoxious last night. I explained how he was still making *Doctor Who* jokes at me when I'd left this morning. "He teases me all the time," I said with a smile. "But that's just him. I know if it came down to it, he'd have my back."

Logan told me about his sister, Beth, how they'd moved with their parents to the States about six years before, how they'd lived together until she'd married last year and now lived just a five-minute drive away. "She owns a bookstore down on West Third," he told me. "I help her out there on Sundays to give her a break."

I asked him if he read much, to which he gave a

pointed nod to the far wall. I turned around to see a wall covered floor to ceiling in books. I snorted, amused at the city library in his living room. "I take it that's a yes."

Smiling, he stood up and took our empty plates into the kitchen. I put the cushions back on the sofa, then packed up the empty containers and followed him, straightening out the kinks in my back and legs from sitting on the floor. We cleaned up, and the conversation didn't stop. He asked me about work, which job site I was currently working on, and what the guys I worked with were like.

"They're okay," I answered honestly. "We work in crews of four or five, and they're not too bad. Some don't like that I'm gay but don't say anything. The others don't care."

He looked at me thoughtfully. "How did they find out?"

"I told them," I answered. "Not gonna lie about it. They were always talking about girls and getting laid or whatever, and they asked me about my weekend score, so I told them."

Logan stared at me, confused. "Score?"

"Oh." I smiled. "Latest conquest, you know..." I cringed. "Anyway, I told them I met some guy at a bar and took him home."

"Oh." Logan blinked again, clearly shocked, and cleared his throat. "What did they say?"

"Not much they could say. I just looked them in the eye and told them I was gay. No big deal."

Logan's eyes widened slightly, and he seemed oddly impressed. "Wow." He grabbed two bottles of water and walked back into the living room, this time sitting on the sofa.

I glanced at him, a little perplexed by his reaction. Sitting down beside him, I asked, "What about you?"

"Oh," he said, the corner of his lips pulled downward. "I've never had to really *tell* anyone. Most people presume I'm gay." Then he pushed his glasses up his nose and looked at me. "I don't mind. It's just me. I'm soft-spoken, well-dressed, a little feminine..."

Feminine...

I frowned. "Don't know about *feminine*, but you're cute."

His mouth fell open, disbelievingly. He obviously didn't get compliments very often.

I laughed. "Don't be so shocked. You are."

He stared at me with wide eyes and pink cheeks, and his mouth snapped shut.

I smiled at him and shook my head. When I reached out to grab the *Doctor Who* DVDs, his hand on my arm stopped me. My gaze went from his long fingers on my forearm to his face. He must have seen my questioning look.

"Why are you here?"

I was surprised at his question. "What?"

He swallowed nervously. "Why are you here?" he repeated softly. "With me? I mean, you don't seem the type to be interested in guys like me."

I didn't know what to say. I didn't know the answer. I'd never been interested in his type, in the quiet, geeky type, so what *was* I doing there? I stared at him, my eyes darting between his, and I shrugged uncertainly. "I don't know," I told him, hoping he could see the honesty in my eyes. "There's something about you... I can't stop thinking about you."

He blinked again. It was obviously something he did

often. This time the blush on his cheeks crept down his neck. "Oh," he whispered.

We stared at each other for a moment, and I found myself leaning in towards him. I licked my lips, and my voice was just a murmur. "Can I kiss you?"

His breath caught. But he nodded.

So I did.

I leaned in and watched his eyes flutter closed as I pressed my lips to his. The kiss was soft and serene, contradicted by the erratic thumping of my heart.

I didn't move to deepen the kiss. I just pressed my lips to his again and again, pulling his bottom lip in between mine. His breath stuttered, and when his eyes slowly opened, they were a stormy gray.

But then I accidentally bumped his glasses with my nose, and I smiled. He was still a little kiss-drunk, and when I pulled back from him, his hand cupped my jaw.

Then it was my eyes that widened, and it was my breath that caught as he kissed me again, deeper, surer, harder. His mouth opened mine, and he licked my bottom lip before softly sliding into my mouth.

It was the most sensual kiss. The hairs on the back of my neck stood on end, my eyes rolled back, and my skin warmed all over.

He tilted our faces and somehow deepened the kiss further. His gentle hands were on my face, holding me to him as his lips, mouth, as *he* consumed me. His tongue teased and twirled against mine. His taste was so enticing, his lips so soft but so sure.

God, he made me moan.

Then he hummed the sweetest sound before slowing the kiss to a stop. When I opened my eyes, it took a moment for me to focus. His face was still close. He seemed as dazed as me.

"Holy shit, Logan," I whispered, breathing in raggedly. "Where did you learn to kiss like that?"

He blushed again and licked his lips. He didn't answer my question—he just smiled.

We were still so close on his sofa, our sides pressed against each other, my face turned towards him. This time I slid my hand along his jaw and made him look at me, our lips almost touching. "Kiss me again," I murmured. "Please."

So he pulled off his glasses and kissed me.

Fucking hell, did he kiss me.

For a quiet, book-loving guy, his strength surprised me. He sure as hell wasn't timid. Without breaking the kiss, he moved up onto his knees, and leaning one knee over my thighs, he straddled me.

My surprise only seemed to spur him on. He pushed my head back onto the sofa with his mouth as he kissed me harder, deeper. He ground his hips onto my lap, making me moan again at the contact.

My cock was straining against my jeans, seeking some kind of friction—any kind of friction. My hips were rising to meet him as he ground down on me and his hands raked my hair.

I was so hard. I was so close to coming.

I gripped his hips and panted into his mouth, "Logan... stop."

He kept his face against mine while he caught his breath, but he kept his eyes closed. He wouldn't look at me.

"Hey," I said, still out of breath. I cupped his face, feeling his soft skin in my hands. I looked at his swollen lips, at his hurt, dark gray eyes. When he tried to pull away from me, I held him tighter. "Hey," I said again, forcing him to look at me. "We should slow down."

"Why?" he asked me, searching my eyes. "Because I'm not your *type*?"

"Ah, no," I told him honestly. "'Cause you're about to make me come."

"Oh," he said with a snort and finally a smile.

I lifted my head off the back of the sofa and pecked his lips with mine. "So damn sexy," I murmured. "You have no idea how sexy you are."

"Yeah, right," he laughed, dismissing me. Embarrassed, he swung his leg over, off me. "I got a bit carried away."

I kept his face near mine, our foreheads touching, and turned my body to face him better. "I reckon you did, yeah," I said with a smile. "Not that I'm complaining."

He sighed and rested his head on my shoulder, and after a little while, he asked, "Did you want to watch *Doctor Who* now?"

No. What I wanted to do was to strip us both naked and bury myself inside him. But I answered politely, "Sure."

CHAPTER FOUR

I SAT sideways on the sofa so my knees were kind of resting near his thigh, and I ignored my hard-on and the ache in my balls. And we watched *Doctor Who*.

Never in a million years would I have thought that'd be something I'd ever do.

Not that I remember much of what I saw. I was too busy wishing my dick was free from my jeans. I shifted in my seat, trying to find the most comfortable spot, but realized sitting so close to him, our legs still touching, didn't exactly help.

"Are you okay?" Logan asked. He had his glasses back on. "You seem a little distracted."

"I'm fine," I lied. I picked up my empty water bottle. "Though I could use another drink."

"Oh, sure," he said, getting up quickly and heading for the kitchen.

Not having any clue what Doctor Who was up to, I followed him. "Oh," I said, looking at the dining table. "I completely forgot about my accounts! Should we do that now?"

Logan smiled at me. "Uh, no, it's okay. I'll do them."

"We could do them now," I said, looking outside to the darkening sky. "It's not that late."

"No, really," he insisted. "I can take some of it with me tomorrow when I go to the bookstore. It's usually quiet."

"Oh," I said with an understanding nod. "Am I really that bad at keeping books?"

Logan laughed and handed me another bottle of water. "No…" Then he bit his lip and shrugged. "Well, yeah, kind of."

My mouth fell open, but I laughed. "Thanks a lot!"

Logan chuckled at my expression, and I told him comments like those would cost him dinner.

His smile turned into a smirk. "Deal."

A new episode of *Doctor Who* started, and Logan took my hand, leading me back to the sofa. Yes, he was the quiet one, the *feminine* one, as he'd called himself, but he was totally taking the lead.

And I didn't mind one little bit.

As the new episode started, a new character came on the screen, taking me to new levels of interest in *Doctor Who*. "Mmm, who's that?"

Logan stared at me and blinked. His tone told me he wasn't overly impressed. "Captain Jack."

"Is there something wrong with him?" I asked genuinely. "Because he's hot."

Logan rolled his eyes but fought a smile. "Everyone loves him."

"He's hotter than the Doctor."

Looking at me, Logan gasped, astounded that I could possibly say such a thing.

I laughed at him, then shrugged. "What?"

"What's wrong with the Doctor?" he asked with smiling eyes.

"Absolutely nothing," I answered, leaning towards him. "As it happens, tall, lean, very smart English guys seem to be a new favorite."

"Nice save." He grinned and leaned over as though about to kiss me. But he didn't. He fisted my shirt and pulled me with him as he lay back down on the sofa until I was lying on top of him. In one movement, I was between his legs, my hips aligned with his, my face directly above his.

My eyes widened. "Logan…"

He smiled. "What? Was that too direct for you?"

"Uh, no," I said, shaking my head a little. "You just keep surprising me."

His smile faded, then he was serious. "I don't know what it is about you," he said, biting his lip. "You're really not the type of guy I'm used to being around. But I'm… intrigued."

I rested on my forearms, framing his face with my hands. I traced my thumbs across his pale cheeks and smiled at him, pleased he was as confounded by this thing between us as I was. "I was thinking the same thing." I pecked his lips chastely. "But yes, intrigued."

"You don't seem to mind," he said, pushing his hips up into mine. He could feel how aroused I was, as much as I could feel how turned on he was. I moaned, and he smiled at me. "Mmm, didn't think so."

Then I kissed him, hard. For the second time that day, he took his glasses off and threw them on the coffee table so he could kiss me properly. And God, this man could kiss.

I led this time, plunging my tongue into his mouth while my hips pushed him into the sofa. His hands were in my hair, down my back, over my ass, everywhere. He hooked his feet around my legs while he rocked his hips into mine.

He was everywhere—his touch, his scent, his taste, the feel of his hardened cock through his jeans, his tongue in my mouth, his long, slender fingers raking over my body…

God, my senses were on overload. And it wasn't enough.

I pulled my mouth from his, only to pull my shirt off. His eyes went wide as he took in my naked chest, my toned shoulders, and muscled arms, and he licked his lips before pulling my face back to his.

This time his hands skimmed over my skin. And it still wasn't enough.

I sat back on my haunches and pulled his vest off first, then pulled his T-shirt over his head. His pale, lean torso looked even whiter against the dark leather sofa. There were no ripped abs, no tanned pecs like the guys I normally picked up. Logan was slender and trim with cream-colored skin.

He was… he was beautiful.

I leaned down and tasted the skin on his chest, nipping and licking as I went. I took his nipple between my lips, and when I flicked it with my tongue, he arched upwards and moaned. And the sound of his desire jolted straight to my cock.

I lapped at his pale skin, gently biting his other nipple, making him gasp. He dug his fingers into my hair, guiding me, luring me back up his neck. I kissed along his jaw until I found his lips, his mouth, his tongue.

Then he moaned into my mouth. And I was done for. I pulled back from him, only to undo the fly of my jeans and pull my engorged cock out. I was aching so fucking bad. I pumped myself a few times to ease the pressure before Logan's long, slender fingers wrapped around me. He squeezed me and pumped me. I almost came right then.

I quickly undid the button-fly of his jeans and slid my

hand under the elastic of his briefs. I wrapped my hand around his silky smooth shaft and pulled it free from his clothes.

His cock was long. Longer than mine but not as thick. He was smooth and uncut. It made my mouth water.

I wanted to lick him, suck him. I wanted to taste him. But Logan soon had his other hand around his own cock and started to slide our lengths together. My cock against his, rubbing, sliding, thrusting.

My head fell forward and I groaned. "So good. You feel so good."

He let go of his dick and started to pump mine. Between panted breaths, he said, "I want to watch you come."

"Oh God." I bucked into his fist. Knowing my orgasm was close, I grabbed his cock and started to pull and squeeze.

His eyes rolled back. "Oh, yes. Just like that." Then his hips jerked, and with his jaw clenched, he threw his head back, exposing his corded neck. His cock throbbed in my hand before spilling onto his stomach.

His whole body tensed underneath me, jerking and writhing as his orgasm took hold of him. It was so fucking hot to watch. It was one of the most erotic things I'd ever seen.

Watching him made me come. I batted his hand off my cock and quickly pumped myself. Pleasure exploded inside me, hurtling through every cell of my body, and my orgasm shot hot and thick onto the man beneath me.

Logan. Fuck.

I all but collapsed on top of him, smearing our messes between us. I tried to keep my weight off him, but I couldn't move my boneless body. His legs soon wrapped around me, his fingers were in my hair, and he was kissing my neck and shoulder—any place he could reach—while the room spun around me.

I kept thinking I should get up, I should move. And apart from being physically unable to, I just really didn't want to move, not an inch. And by the way Logan held onto me, I figured he didn't want me to either.

But eventually we had to, and it was Logan who moved first. "We should get cleaned up," he said.

I worried things might be a little awkward between us, considering how hot and heavy it had gotten between us so fast. I rested my still-foggy head on my bent arm so I could look at his face, to see if he regretted what we'd just done.

He smiled lazily at me. "We forgot about dinner. Are you hungry?" And my stomach growled right on cue. So much for awkward. Logan threw his head back and laughed, wriggling his way out from under me. "Don't move," he said with a grin. "I'll be right back."

Move? Who was he kidding? I was still so sated I could barely lift my own arm. I did manage to tuck my dick back into my briefs, but he was soon back with a warm cloth, and after we'd cleaned up, we ordered dinner.

We finished watching *Doctor Who* while we ate. Logan explained things as we watched, and we talked and laughed until after midnight. I didn't want to leave, and I told him that. He bit his lip and told me I was welcome to stay.

"I don't think that's a good idea," I told him quietly. I knew what his offer was implying—he wanted us in bed together. "I mean, I think it's a *great* idea," I clarified quickly. "Next time…"

He pouted playfully, so I kissed him and asked, "Can I see you tomorrow?"

"I have to work at my sister's shop," he explained.

"Can I call you tomorrow night?"

He smiled and nodded. "I'd like that."

I pecked his lips again at the door and smiled all the way home.

CHAPTER FIVE

TIM GRINNED AT ME. "Right then, who is he?"

It was too early for his shit. "Who's who?"

"Don't play dumbass with me, Brent," he said, folding his arms across his chest. "You stayed at home Friday night to watch some sci-fi crap, and you left yesterday before lunch and didn't get home till God knows when. Who's the guy?"

I rolled my eyes and sipped my coffee. There was no point in lying to him. He'd know I was lying anyway. "Remember how I had an appointment to see the new accountant on Friday?"

"Yeah."

"Well, that's him."

Tim blinked. "That's who?"

"The guy I'm seeing."

"For your taxes?"

"No, dumbass." I rolled my eyes. Then I amended my statement. "Well, yes, for that too. But he's the one I spent yesterday with."

Tim stared at me for a long while before he blinked again. "You're seeing the bean-counter?"

"Don't call him that."

"That's what *you* were calling him!"

"That was before I met him, when I thought I was going to see some geriatric, boring old fart."

"So, he's not old?"

I shook my head. "Same age as me."

"But he's an accountant?" Tim asked again. "As in, not the athletic, meat-headed guys you normally bring home?"

I laughed. "No. He's not like that at all. He's soft-spoken, British accent, glasses."

"Holy shit!" The look on Tim's face was priceless.

I laughed at him. "Don't worry. I'm just as surprised as you."

"Are you going to see him again?"

I nodded. "I sure hope so."

"Holy shit!"

"I know, it's weird," I admitted with a smile.

"When do I get to meet him?"

I looked at him, horrified. "I don't want to scare him!"

Tim pretended to be offended, but he really just found it funny. He asked a few more questions, then to get the topic off me and Logan, I asked about what the guys had been up to on Friday night, if I'd missed anything.

Of course I hadn't. Same old stories, same old shit. Saul and Marty were good buddies, but nothing with them changed too quickly. They'd wondered where I was, of course—Marty, in particular, was more curious, as always —and Tim *swore* he hadn't told them I was being a loser at home by myself, jerking off over *Doctor Who*.

I rolled my eyes at him. "I didn't jerk off… well, not over *Doctor Who*."

Tim laughed. "Are you seeing him today?"

"No, but I'll give him a call tonight."

———

I DID CALL him later that night, and we chatted for over an hour. And we did the same on Monday and Tuesday nights too. Talking with him was so easy. We talked about our friends, work, and what had been going on in the world.

Though it was not usually something I talked about much, I told him how I'd lived with my grandma for most of my teenage years until she'd passed away and I'd moved in with Tim. He didn't ask any questions, thankfully, and he told me a little about his hometown in England and how he'd moved to the States with his parents and sister.

I asked him if he missed it, and his reply was an emphatic no. But it was obviously not something he wanted to delve into, so I changed the subject.

He saw the world so differently from me, and although he said he wasn't, he was so much smarter than me. His insight and perspective were fascinating to me. I saw things in black and white and never really thought too much of anything outside of my own life. He was so much more knowledgeable about *everything*. His thoughts were calculated and intelligent, yet he seemed equally absorbed in things I talked about.

And before we ended our phone conversation on Tuesday, I asked if I could see him the next night. I might have bribed him with promises of dinner, but he answered with, "I'd like that."

And when I got to his place on Wednesday, I could hear him talking on the other side of the door. I knocked anyway, and he opened the door with a smile and his phone to his ear. I stepped inside the doorway, and ignoring the fact that he was talking to someone else, I kissed him soundly before walking in.

He laughed into the phone. "No, Beth, I have to go. He's here."

Oh. He's here…

He clicked off the call and smiled as he kissed me again. "My sister was playing twenty questions."

"You told her about me?" I asked, though it was more a statement than a question.

"Um… yes," he answered hesitantly, pushing his glasses up on his nose.

I smiled. "It's okay, Logan," I told him. "I told Tim about you too."

"You did?" His eyes widened in surprise and he blinked.

Nodding, I smiled at him. "I sure did." I took his face in my hands and kissed him deeper this time, savoring the feel of his soft lips, the sweet taste of his mouth. He sighed into the kiss, melting into me. Not breaking the kiss, I slid my arms around him and pulled him against me, my body acutely aware of how he fit against me.

I'd only been near him for a minute, and I already wanted him. Figuring I'd better pace myself, I slowed the kiss. When I pulled my mouth from him, I smiled at the kiss-drunk look on his face and straightened his glasses for him. He chuckled, a little embarrassed.

I noticed then that the dining table was cleared of all my receipts and papers. "Oh, you've finished with my accounts?"

Logan smiled, but it was hardly genuine. The look confused me, but before I could comment, he said, "No, I, um, I've sorted all the paperwork into a general ledger. I'll have more done tomorrow."

"I didn't mean you should have it done by now," I told

him quickly, worried I'd offended him. "It just means we don't have to eat sitting on the floor."

Knowing then that I wasn't teasing him for not doing his job, Logan smiled properly.

"Anyway," I went on to say, "I thought we could go out for dinner."

"Really?"

"Sure. I mean, only if you want to."

He looked surprised. "Um, yeah. Sure."

I looked down and waved my hand at my jeans and T-shirt. "Know anywhere close by where this is good enough?"

"You look fine," he said softly.

"Well, I did iron my shirt," I boasted proudly.

Logan smiled warmly. "Do that often?"

"Um, only on special occasions." I grinned. "Which is not very often." I looked at his neatly pressed charcoal dress pants, neat black shirt, and light-gray vest. "You iron everything, don't you?"

He pouted playfully. "Yes."

I laughed and shook my head, marveling at just how different we were. I pecked his lips. "Come on. I'm starving."

We soon found a small café where we settled in for dinner and easy conversation. I kept waiting for us to run out of things to talk about, considering how opposite we were, but it never happened. The conversation between us never stopped.

We'd finished our main course and were having coffee when Logan's eyes kept darting around the room. I followed his gaze. There were other people having dinner, but nothing looked out of the ordinary. I couldn't see anyone staring at us, but it wouldn't be the first time small-minded people had found two guys together offensive. "What's wrong? Are people looking at us?"

"No," he answered quietly. "I'm just wary, you know?"

I frowned at him and put down my coffee. "Did something happen to you?"

His lips twisted into a thoughtful pout, as though he was choosing his words carefully. "Just the usual school and university stuff, you know…"

"No. I don't know."

Logan smiled sadly and nodded. "Well, you probably wouldn't. You're a big guy, played football…" He said the word as though it tasted bad. "And I was the little kid, the geek with glasses in the chess club. Add gay to that…"

He didn't have to finish.

"I'm sorry," I said, though I knew they were such inadequate words.

He smiled ruefully. "It's not your fault."

I took a deep breath. "Did your parents support you?"

He gave me a small smile. "Yeah, my family was fine. It was just everyone else who wasn't."

The complete opposite of me. We *really* were so very different.

Before he could ask me about my family, I reached out across the table and slid my hand over his. "Well, I'd like to see someone say something to you now," I told him. I was going to add "while I'm with you" but stopped short. I looked around the room again. "If anyone here has a problem with us, with this"—I held up our joined hands—"they can speak to me about it."

He smiled and blushed, silently pleased with my protective comment.

"Logan," I said his name gently, "for what it's worth, I've had my share of people who didn't agree with"—I searched for the right word—"my sexuality." I lifted the hand not holding his and bent my nose, proving it had been broken. Twice. "See? Battle scars," I said, trying to lighten the conversation. But then I told him, "Logan, if someone does say something, anything to you, then just let me know."

"I don't need a babysitter," he said, biting his lip.

I gasped, faking offense. "I'll have you know, there's a difference between babysitting and defending one's honor with valor."

He smiled then. "You'd do that for me."

"Yes."

On the table, his fingers curled around mine, and he stared at me. His eyes searched mine for the longest moment, then he swallowed. "I think we should go home."

I couldn't help but smile. "I think so too."

I knew what he was asking, and my dick came to life.

I wanted him.

And we both knew, when we got back to his place, I would have him.

CHAPTER SIX

———————

HE CERTAINLY DIDN'T WASTE time. We were no sooner through his front door than he took my hand and, without another word, led me to his bedroom. It was darkened, but my eyes soon adjusted. I didn't want to miss a thing.

He walked us over to his bedside table, found a condom and lube, and threw them on the bed. The muted light only made him look even more beautiful. His dark hair looked pitch black, his pale skin almost white.

He took his glasses off and looked at me, his eyes a little out of focus. I cupped his face in my hands, rested his forehead against mine, and searched his eyes. I watched for any sign of hesitation, but there was none.

He wanted this. He wanted me.

He wanted me as much as I wanted him.

I was so turned on, hard and aching. But it was unhurried between us, savored. I took my time kissing him, undressing him, adoring him, prepping him.

His pale, lithe body writhed under me. His moans

turned to words of "more" and "please, please, now, please."

I sheathed myself, and lifting and spreading his legs, I pressed my cock against his ready hole. I leaned over him, looking for any flicker of doubt in his eyes.

His only response was to lift his legs higher, offering himself to me, urging me to please, please push into him, where he wanted me, needed me. Keeping his eyes open, he lifted his head off the bed and kissed me. "Brent," he murmured. "Please."

So inch by exquisite inch, I gave him what he so desperately wanted.

I pushed in oh so slowly until I could go no farther, keeping my lips on his, kissing him softly. Logan's knees were bent up near my chest, and my hips were flush on his ass.

I was so far inside him. It was so hot, so tight. So right.

"Oh God," he groaned, low in his throat. "Move for me, baby."

I rocked my hips, thrusting long and slow.

Logan gasped and groaned as I moved inside him. His legs wrapped around me, pinning me to him, in him. He rocked us, setting the pace, thrusting his hips so my cock slid in and out of him, as *he* wanted, as *he* needed.

I wanted to watch my cock slide into him, but I needed to kiss him even more. Leaning over him, I touched his face before I fused my mouth to his, teasing him with my tongue.

One of his hands fisted in my hair, making me moan, and his other hand slipped in between us. He pumped himself, pushing his hips up to meet my thrusts in time with his hand.

I might have been topping him, but so help me God, he was in charge. He set the pace.

He led me, and all I could do was follow.

Then he started to buck underneath me, groaning and squeezing. His head pushed back, and his hand pumped faster, faster, harder. I was so deep in him, fueling his fire.

He convulsed under me one last time, and with a strangled groan, he came. I stared in wonder as his orgasm surged through him, erupting hot and wet between us.

So beautiful. So fucking beautiful.

Watching him, feeling him, being inside him while he unraveled beneath me, brought me to the edge. When he held my face and he said, "Come, baby, come," it did me in.

My senses came back to me with the feel of long slender fingers tracing feather-light patterns on my cheeks and in my hair. I opened my eyes to find Logan barely an inch from my face. His eyes were heavy-lidded, and he had a blissful smirk. "Hey."

"Hey." My voice croaked. Then I mumbled, "Jesus, what did you do to me?"

He hummed and smiled, a little smugly. I kissed him. "Don't go anywhere," I told him, getting off the bed. Walking into the bathroom, I discarded the condom and took a warm, wet cloth to use to clean us both up.

Logan hadn't moved and was still lying on his side. I crawled up his body, washing him down, kissing his damp skin as I went. I rolled him onto his back, wiped him clean, kissed his hip, his stomach, his ribs, collarbone, and finally his jaw and lips.

He smiled, but his eyes weren't focusing on me properly. "Um, Logan?" I asked, pulling his bottom lip between mine.

"Mmm?"

"Can I ask you something?"

"Mm-hmm," he hummed again, and still his eyes were dancing all over my face.

"Can you see without your glasses?"

He grinned. "No. Not a thing."

I collapsed beside him, laughing into a pillow before reaching over to his bedside table. I turned on the lamp and grabbed his glasses, then lining them up, I slid them on his nose. "How's that?"

"Much better."

I scanned his face and tapped the heavy-framed glasses. "I like these," I told him. "They suit you."

He blushed and bit down on his bottom lip. I chuckled at his sudden shyness, considering what we'd just done, and rolled us over, pulling him into my arms. I kissed the side of his head, then his cheek. I'd never been one to cuddle or to even stay in someone else's bed after sex, but with him, with Logan, I didn't want to leave.

I didn't let myself dwell on that or how new and odd this was. This delicate man in my arms felt so right. I didn't want to question it. I just wanted to enjoy it.

We lay like that, in silence, for a while, and when I told him I wished I didn't have to leave, his response was simple.

"Then stay."

I rubbed his back and smiled. "I have to be at work by six-thirty. Not like those lazy accountants who have till nine."

He chuckled quietly, then sighed contentedly.

I traced my fingers up his spine. "Can I see you tomorrow?"

He leaned up on my chest and looked at me for a long moment. He nodded. "I'd like that."

I smiled and leaned up to kiss him. "Me too."

My head fell back on the pillow and his finger traced

my eyebrow and across my cheek. His voice was quiet but sure. "I've never known anyone like you."

I smiled. "What? Don't you have cute electrician who keep their taxes in an old shoebox in to see you every day?"

He grinned and shook his head, but I knew what he meant. We were very different. I wasn't his usual type any more than he was mine. I didn't want it to be an issue between us. "But we're good, aren't we?" I asked, suddenly very nervous at what he would answer.

But he nodded and agreed with a whispered, "Yeah, we're good." He kissed my chest before lying back down on me.

I stared at the ceiling and ran my hand over the soft skin on his back. "For what it's worth, Logan," I admitted quietly, "I've never known anyone like you either."

———

I DID SEE him the next night. Only this time we ended up naked on his bed, lying on our sides, giving mutual blow jobs.

I needed to taste him. I needed to have him in my mouth.

Slipping the head of his cock between my lips, I gripped his slim hips and pulled his cock down my throat. I sucked him, cupped his balls, and pumped him while his talented tongue swirled around me. We came only moments apart, and I maneuvered us quickly so I could kiss him, our tastes mingling in our mouths.

We lay naked for a long while, talking and laughing, and eventually got up to eat a late dinner. That was when I told him I wanted him to come to my place the next night.

"Why?"

"Because it's Friday night."

He looked confused. "So?"

I took a deep breath. "I want you to meet Tim." Logan knew all about my roommate, but he was still surprised. "He's been hassling me for information about you," I told him honestly. "And the good thing is, because it's Friday night, he'll go out and leave us alone."

Logan blinked. "Um…"

I smiled. "So if you got to my house around six-ish, you'd meet him just as he's about to leave, and he won't be there to bother us." Then I added, "Or to embarrass me."

Logan chuckled. "He can't be *that* bad."

I snorted incredulously. "The stories I've told you are only the ones that bear repeating and, even then, only very censored."

"Oh." Logan shook his head with a laugh.

"So will you meet him?"

"You really want me to?"

I nodded.

He pushed his glasses up on his nose. "Okay then," he said. I could tell he was nervous, but his smile for the rest of the night was stellar.

CHAPTER SEVEN

GIVEN that I finished work after three, I had about two or so hours before Logan would arrive at my place. That gave me enough time to stop and pick up some dinner, get home, and clean. I cleaned my room, the living room, kitchen, bathroom and even the toilet. Tim stared at me like I'd lost my freakin' mind.

By the time I had the place resembling something other than a pigsty, got out of my dirty work clothes, and showered, Tim was smirking at me.

I looked at his all-knowing, shit-eating grin. "What?"

"Nothing," he replied, still smiling. I stopped and stared at him, so he grinned. "Well, this guy must be something special. You've never cleaned up for anyone before."

"Well, I don't want him to think we live like pigs."

Tim snorted. "But we do live like pigs."

I looked at my housemate. "Well, Logan doesn't. His place is clean and organized and expensive and… and…"

"And *gay?*" he deadpanned.

I rolled my eyes at him. "I just want the place to look nice." I looked around the living room at the old mismatched furniture, and I amended it with, "Well, I want it to look clean."

Tim grinned. "You know, the guys are gonna want to meet this mystery man that's kept you busy the last two Friday nights in a row. That's a first for Brent Kelly."

The corner of my lip pulled downward. "I, um, I don't think Logan's ready for them yet." Then I shrugged. "And I'm pretty sure Marty isn't ready to meet Logan."

Marty. Marty was a good guy, one of the guys we had drinks with. He was bi and had made it pretty clear—several times—he was interested in me. I'd told him I just didn't see him like that and had managed to avoid having that awkward conversation since. He'd watched me for months picking up random men. We all knew he didn't like it, but he never commented. Not to me anyway.

And right then, there was a knock at the door. I looked at the time. Five to six. I looked at Tim and warned him, "Be nice."

I left Tim grinning in the kitchen, and when I opened the door, I smiled as soon as I saw Logan. He was wearing dark blue jeans, a light-gray shirt, and his trademark black vest. A shy smile spread across his lips, and his eyes glittered behind his glasses.

"Hey," I breathed, pressing my lips to his. "Come in."

I shut the door behind him and kissed him again before leading him through the living room to the kitchen, where Tim was still waiting. I was so nervous. I wanted them to get along. I wanted Tim to see Logan how I saw him. I made introductions, and the two men shook hands.

Tim smiled widely. "So you're this Logan I've heard all about?"

Logan looked at me, then back to Tim and smiled nervously. "Brent talks about you as well."

His English accent was soft, and he looked so out of

place. And looking at him, despite his height, he was so pale and small compared to us well-built and tanned electrician. He looked a little intimidated. So I stepped beside him, smiling as I took his hand and gave it a squeeze.

We made small talk for a while. Tim was well-behaved by his standards, but he had an amused smirk the entire time. When Logan asked where the bathroom was and excused himself, Tim stared at me, wide-eyed and on the verge of laughing. Then he whispered, "Brent, my man, he's... he's um... he's nice. But he's a geek."

I blinked at his words, and I'm sure he saw the hurt on my face. I was tempted to say a lot of things—a lot of hurt, offended, fucking angry things—but settled for, "You have yourself a good night."

I turned to leave him, but he grabbed my arm. "Hey, that's not what I meant," he said quietly, truthfully. I knew my best friend well enough to know when he was being honest. Then he said, "I mean, sure, it was a surprise. He's not exactly the type of guy you go for. But that's not what surprised me the most." He shook his head, still wide-eyed. "It was how you looked at him. Jesus, Brent..." Tim shook his head again and poked me in the chest. "You've got it bad."

He smiled at me and lifted his eyebrows, but before he could say anything else, before I could think to answer, Logan walked back into the kitchen. He looked at me nervously, knowing in all likelihood that we'd just been talking about him. I looked at Logan and explained, "Tim was just leaving."

Logan smiled anxiously and bit his lip, so I pulled him toward the fridge. "I thought I could try and cook dinner. Is that okay?"

Tim barked out a laugh, making us turn to look at him.

He was staring at me again. "You, Brent Kelly, are going to *cook*?"

"Shut up," I told him. "I cook… sometimes."

My housemate snorted. "Oh-kay," he said slowly. "Sure you do." Then he looked at Logan. "Good luck with that. Use The Force… or something." Then he held up his hand in the Vulcan salute. "Beam me up, Scotty, or whatever the sci-fi term is for 'good luck and I hope you don't get food poisoning.'"

Logan and I both stared at him. "Oh, for God's sake," I mumbled. Then I looked at Logan and smiled apologetically. "Ignore him. He'll go away soon."

"Yep." Tim rocked back on his heels. "Well, I'll just be heading off now." He grinned at me. "I'm sure Marty will have a hundred questions."

"Tim," I warned. "Please don't."

He chuckled, and Logan looked at me, a little alarmed. "Who's Marty?"

Tim answered. "One of our buddies who has a crush on Brent."

I jumped in quickly, "Yeah, and Brent's not interested in Marty." Then I looked at Logan and shook my head. "I'm not interested in Marty."

Tim laughed. "Everyone knows you're not interested in Marty." Then he shrugged. "Well, except for Marty."

I glared at him. "Aren't you late?"

"Yeah, I'm going." He grinned. "Don't you two do anything I wouldn't do." Then he stopped and thought about what he'd just said. "Actually, I'm not sure that applies to two gay guys."

Ignoring him completely, I took the dish of chicken pieces out of the fridge and showed it to Logan.

"What is it?" he asked.

"Um, the lady at the shop called it chicken something?" I said. "And apparently it needs forty-five minutes in the oven."

I heard Tim laughing as the front door closed behind him, and I sighed loudly. "I'm really sorry about him," I said. "He's a great guy. He just *thinks* he's funny."

Logan smiled. "He was great," he told me and pushed his glasses up on his nose. "I thought it went just fine."

"He was *great*?" I scoffed. "We're talking about the same guy, right?"

Logan smiled shyly and pulled his bottom lip between his teeth. "That was the first time I've been introduced to someone as the date of another man."

"Well, that's the first time I've ever had someone over and introduced them... well, to anyone," I admitted. He looked at me disbelievingly, so I leaned in and kissed him. "I've never really had a boyfriend before, so..."

"Oh." Logan blushed. "Boyfriend..." He turned back to the uncooked chicken. He pushed his glasses up on his nose and tried not to smile. "Um, we better get this into the oven."

I acted like I wasn't embarrassed, then I acted like I knew what I was doing when I tried to put the chicken on a tray and in the oven. I'd seen it done on TV, and the lady at the shop had told me it was fail-safe. Actually, I think the word she used was 'idiot-proof.'

Logan smiled at me as though he found me amusing. But after I got dinner in the oven and cleaned up, I grinned at him proudly. "See? I can cook!"

He threw his head back and laughed. "Do I want to know what we're having with this chicken?"

His smile made me smile. "They have these pre-made salad packs—they're already done," I told him, though I think he might have already known this. "And some fresh-baked rolls. I mean, I know you watch your carbs and all, and you're not a big eater, but I can't live on salad without some kind of bread—"

He kissed me to shut me up. "It's perfect."

I took his face in my hands and kissed him properly, slowly, deeply. And when I finally pulled my lips from his, I showed him what I'd gotten from the sci-fi shop.

"I've created a monster!" Logan exclaimed, shaking his head. I'd bought more *Doctor Who* DVDs and some *Torchwood* DVDs. Logan held up the last DVD and stared at me. "*Predator?*"

I shrugged. "Well, it is science fiction… just with blood and guts and gore. See? American science fiction…" I nodded to the *Predator* DVD, then toward the not-so-crudely-violent *Doctor Who*. "And British science fiction."

He chuckled and pulled me onto the sofa, and in his very sexy English accent, he asked, "So, British or American?"

"British," I said, pressing my lips to his. "Definitely British."

And because I declared the actors better looking, we watched some *Torchwood* first and made out on the sofa until dinner was done. We worked together in the kitchen to get it served up, and funnily enough, it was quite good. I think Logan was pleasantly surprised. I know I certainly was.

I pulled him into my arms on the couch, his head on my chest, as we watched *Doctor Who*. About halfway through an episode, I asked, "So these Daleks conquer entire planets, right?"

"Mm-hmm." He nodded against my chest.

"But they can't even go up steps."

Logan lifted his head and looked at me. His glasses were a little crooked from lying down. He looked… offended.

"Oh, come on." I snorted. "So to escape from these oh-so-terrifying robot-type creatures who are vying for world domination, all the good Doctor had to do was install some stairs?"

Logan's mouth fell open and he scoffed in disbelief. Then his mouth snapped shut and his brow furrowed. "You take that back. They do fly, you know."

He started to lecture me about the Ninth Doctor disproving that theory, but I laughed, and he jumped up, straddled my hips, and pinned my hands to my sides. I could've easily thrown him off. I was twice as strong as him, but I played along. He leaned his forehead on mine and looked down at me, trying not to grin. "No picking on the Doctor."

I laughed again, and leaning up, I kissed him. He pulled my face up and he smashed his mouth to mine. He wiggled his hips forward, settling himself on my groin, rubbing against me as he kissed me. He had me hard in no time, grinding upwards into him while he pressed down on me.

Keeping his hips against mine, I gripped his ass, and in one swift movement, I stood up. He wrapped his legs around me, and he smiled into the kiss. "You're so strong."

I chuckled. "You're so light."

He fisted my hair and he rested his forehead against mine. He wriggled against my hard cock. "Is that a problem?"

"None whatsoever," I told him, and not letting him go or putting him down, I walked us to my room. I walked until my knees hit my bed, and I laid him down on his back. His legs never let me go and I settled between his thighs. "You're so fucking sexy."

He looked at me and shook his head like he thought I was lying.

"You have no idea how sexy you are," I told him, pushing his short brown hair back off his forehead. I touched his glasses, and when his hand came up to remove them, I stopped him. "Leave them on," I told him. "I want you to watch what you do to me."

He gasped quietly and nodded. And when we were both naked, he rolled us over and straddled me. He sheathed me in latex and lube and slowly impaled himself on me.

"Oh, Logan, baby," I gasped. "Oh, fuck."

His pale, slender body sank so perfectly on me. He took all of me, groaning and sighing as he did. I ran my hands all over him, feeling every part I could reach—his soft skin, his pale chest, his thin waist, his taut hips. His long, hard cock slapped my stomach as he thrust himself on me.

"Oh God," he grunted. "You feel so good." For a quiet, shy guy, he talked dirty, and he took charge. I was easily twice as strong as him, but he never hesitated to take what he wanted from me.

Leaning down, he kissed me. His tongue fucked my mouth in rhythm with me fucking his ass. He groaned and moaned, and the sounds he made unleashed fire in my belly. He thrust, fucking me hard and fast until I gripped his hips and screamed through my orgasm.

I came hard, spilling over and over into the condom. My whole body shook as wave after wave of pleasure rolled through me. He moaned as I twitched and throbbed inside him, then he slid off my cock. He knelt over my stomach with his dick in his hand and poured ribbons of hot come across my chest.

With heavy bodies and lazy smiles, we showered, washing each other. I relished soaping him up, running my hands all over him, cleaning him, caring for him. He did the same for me, and we kissed in the shower until the water went cold. We dried off and got back into bed naked. I pulled the covers over us, pulled him into my arms, and closed my eyes.

I couldn't remember ever being so happy or feeling so content. I wondered what it was about this unlikely man in my arms, what it was that had captured me so completely.

I didn't think it was one thing in particular. It was just *him*.

I tightened my arms around him and kissed the top of his head. His soft breathing lulled me into sleep.

CHAPTER EIGHT

USED TO EARLY MORNINGS, I woke before Logan and decided to put his morning wood to good use. I wiggled down under the covers, took his rigid length in my hand, and licked him from base to tip. He moaned. Then I took him in fully, sliding my wet mouth up and down, flicking his tip with my tongue on every pass.

He jerked awake. "Jesus!"

I grinned at him from under the blanket. "Morning, baby."

He fell back against the pillow, and I went back to his waiting cock. His fingers soon found my hair, guiding me as he wanted me, needed me. I cupped his balls in my hand, stopping only to lick and suck on them, then returning my attention to his leaking slit.

"Oh, fuck," he groaned, his voice still thick from sleep. "Brent, baby, gonna come."

So I slid my mouth over him as far as I could and pumped the base, feeling him twitch and pulse before he spurted his seed down my throat. He groaned loudly through his release, and his whole body trembled while he fisted the sheets at his side.

His moan became a chuckle and a blissful, sated grin covered his face. I crawled up his body and fell back onto my side of the bed. His hooded eyes, sans glasses, looked in my general direction. "Your turn," he croaked.

"No," I told him happily, "that was just for you."

He blinked at me a few times, trying to focus on me, then he settled back against his pillow. His blissful smirk returned, and he sighed. "What time is it?"

"Uh, quarter to eight."

He groaned. "Not that I mind being woken up by your mouth," he said, rubbing his eyes. "But that's far too early for a Saturday."

I chuckled and leaned over him, collecting his glasses off the bedside table and handing them to him. He smiled and I rolled out of bed. "Come on, I'll make you coffee."

I threw on my jeans from the night before and walked shirtless into the kitchen. Not a moment later, Logan joined me, wearing his jeans and shirt.

I looked up from the coffee mugs. "No vest?" I asked him.

He looked at my naked torso and grinned. "No shirt?"

I grinned and shrugged. "I like your vests, by the way," I told him. "They suit you."

"I like you without a shirt," he said with a suggestive flicker of his eyebrow.

I grinned at him again, and our playful morning banter continued well into our second cup of coffee until a very disheveled Tim stumbled into the kitchen.

He wore only his boxers and what looked like a monster hangover. We were silent as we watched him pour himself a cup of coffee and sip it while he scratched his ass. "Mornin'," he croaked.

I tried not to laugh. "Good morning," I said, probably louder than required. Tim shot me a dark look and I smiled at him. "Headache?"

He groaned. And just then, a slim, nameless brunette woman walked from his room through the kitchen, gave Tim a smile, and kept walking presumably to the front door. She left without so much as a word.

Logan's eyes widened, and he smiled behind his coffee mug. I looked at Tim and he just sipped his coffee and shrugged.

Then out walked a full-figured blonde woman, smiling at us three men in the kitchen. "Bye, Tim." She giggled and waved as she left.

"Bye," Tim called out after her.

Logan's mouth was hanging open and his eyes were wide. He was clearly shocked and somewhat amused. His gaze darted to me, and I looked at Tim and sighed. "Good night, huh?"

Tim smiled and nodded. Logan looked at me, then back towards Tim's bedroom door. "It's like those little cars at the circus," he said.

I laughed, and Tim chuckled into his coffee.

"Anyone else crammed in there?" Logan asked with a smile.

"Nah," Tim laughed. "Slow night."

I was still chuckling when I leaned in and kissed the side of Logan's head. Tim looked at me and smiled approvingly at Logan's sense of humor, put his coffee down, then stretched with a yawn and groan. "What you guys doing today?"

I looked at Logan and shrugged, unsure.

He looked at Tim and told him, "I'm taking Brent shopping for a laptop."

I looked at Logan, like I didn't understand a word he'd said. "You're what?"

He smiled. "No more shoebox of accounts for you, I'm afraid."

I grimaced. "But I… I can't… I'm no good with computers."

"I'll teach you," he said simply. Then he sighed and gave me a sympathetic nod. "You need a laptop," he repeated. "It will save you time and money if you keep accounts electronically, and you can use it as a tax deduction."

"But I…" I started to protest, and Logan got off the stool at the breakfast bar and patted my hand.

"You'll be fine. The twenty-first century won't bite."

Tim snorted out a laugh, and I shot him a scathing glance. But knowing Logan wasn't going to see my logic, I needed a different approach. I ran my thumb across his jaw, leaned in, and whispered low and dirty in his ear, "I had better plans for us today. I was going to see how many times I could make you come."

He gasped, and his eyes flickered to my housemate, who was watching us, amused.

I pulled Logan's chin between my thumb and forefinger, making him look at me. "My plan sounds much better."

Logan blushed seven shades of pink, but he licked his lips and nodded. "Then we'll, um, we can…" He cleared his throat. "We could always go laptop shopping during the week."

Tim laughed and put his empty cup in the sink. "Brent, buddy, you only bought yourself some time." He clapped me on the shoulder and said, "Don't think you'll be getting out of that one." Then Tim looked at Logan, who was almost tucked into my side, smiled, and told him, "I didn't hear what he whispered to you, but whatever it was, make sure he delivers."

Logan blushed again and chuckled into my skin, hiding his face as he mumbled, "I'm sure he will."

Tim laughed as he walked out of the kitchen and back into his room. "I'm going back to bed."

I smiled at Logan. "So are we." I took our coffee cups and put them in the sink, then took his hand and led him to my room where I told him, "I've got promises to deliver, and you've only come once so far today."

I soon remedied that, making it twice before nine in the morning. I undid his jeans, freeing his hardening cock, and I pumped him good and hard while I whispered delicious things in his ear.

He was a panting, mumbling mess as he fumbled with my jeans and started to stroke me. I soon took both our cocks in my hand, pumping and sliding them together. God, the feel of his cock pressed against mine, hot and hard, as I watched him bask in the sensation, the pleasure. I could feel him swell and lurch before his body convulsed, spurting hot come over his stomach, and not a moment later, I did the same.

I collapsed over him, rolling us to our sides, keeping him in my arms, my body thoroughly spent. I could feel him smiling into my neck.

"Come on," I sighed, then rolled off the bed, playfully smacking his ass. "Shower time."

He stared at me with nothing on but his glasses and a sated smile. "That's twice already."

I grinned at him. "And I'm nowhere near done with you yet."

———

"BRENT, BABY," Logan mumbled, still trying to catch his breath. "I don't think I can come anymore today."

I chuckled. "I'll be the judge of that."

We'd arrived at his place and had had an early lunch, only to end up in his bed in a sixty-nine, giving mutual blow jobs. He really did have a very talented mouth.

I traced my fingers around his lips. "That was only number three for the day," I informed him with a nod. "I'm certain there's at least another one to go."

His head fell back against his pillow, and he laughed with a groan, just as his cell phone rang.

He slid off the bed to find his jeans and pulled out his phone. He squinted at the screen, shrugged because he couldn't read it without his glasses, but answered anyway. "Hello?"

I chuckled at him and crawled across the bed to his bedside table and collected his glasses. He was trying to put his boxer briefs back on with one hand, talking to someone who I soon realized was his sister. "Beth, can this wait?"

Grinning, I carefully slid the thick black frames into place on his face and pecked his lips with mine. Figuring I'd give him some privacy, I put on my briefs and walked out to the living room. I could hear him trying to convince his sister about something to do with her shop, saying something about the landlord's responsibilities, and not wanting to eavesdrop, I walked over to his bookcase.

Jesus, there must have been hundreds of books—hardcovers, paperbacks, history, fiction, reference books, poetry. You name it, it was there. Even though they seemed to be in some kind of order, I didn't even know where to start. Until one title caught my eye. *Treasure Island.*

God, I hadn't read that since I was little. My mom had read it to me…

"Sorry about that," Logan said beside me. "It was Beth."

"Everything okay?"

He sighed. "The landlord's supposed to have fixed something and hasn't," he said. Then added, "Or won't."

"What needs fixing?" I asked. "Maybe I could have a look at it for you."

He shook his head. "Oh, no. Don't worry about it."

"Logan, I don't mind," I said with a smile. "I can stop by tomorrow while you're working and take a look. At least I might be able to tell you what the problem is."

"It's the back storage room. I think it's the wiring," he said, unsure.

I snorted. "Logan, baby, wiring is what I do."

His face fell. "That's why I didn't want to say anything. I didn't want you to think I—"

I pressed my fingers to his mouth to shush him. His eyes were wide behind his glasses, so I replaced my fingers with my lips, kissing him softly. "Call your sister and tell her you'll have someone take a look at it tomorrow for her."

He smiled, held his phone up, and texted her instead, while I went back to studying his bookshelves.

"Have you read all these?" I asked.

He nodded. "Some a few times," he said. "Do you read?"

"Um, I read job cards at work and the takeout menus for dinner," I told him with an embarrassed laugh. "But I don't think they count."

Logan chuckled. "No, I don't think they do."

I smiled and turned back to the books. I reached out and took *Treasure Island*, looking over the familiar cover. "This used to be my favorite when I was a kid."

"Take it and read it again."

"Um…" I shook my head. I wasn't sure I could explain what the book itself meant, what childhood memories were attached to it. "I, um…"

Logan took the book out of my hand, and grabbing my arm, he led me back to his room. He climbed onto his bed, wearing only his boxer briefs and glasses, put *Treasure Island* on my pillow, and patted the bed beside him.

He pulled his pillow up against the headboard, grabbed his own book off the bedside table, and grinned at me. "I've always wanted to lie in bed with another man and just read," he said quietly. "Not your average fantasy, I know."

I smiled at him, crawled up the bed, and kissed him right on the lips. "You're such a nerd." I picked up the book and lay down beside him. He smiled sheepishly at me before opening his book, and for the next few minutes, he read quietly, while I just turned the book over in my hands.

"We don't have to read if you don't want to."

I looked up at him, then back to the unopened book I was holding. "It's not that… It's just… it's just this book…" I trailed off, not too comfortable in discussing this part of my life.

Logan closed his book and put it down on the bed. Then he did the darnedest thing. He took the book out of my hands, opened it to the beginning, and started to read to me.

Out loud. Just like my mom used to do.

His voice was soft, musical, and his accent made it sound somehow even better. I found myself lying down on my side next to him, watching him, listening to him, mesmerized by him. Only when he'd read the entire first chapter did he stop and look over at me. I smiled at him and told him softly, "My mom used to read this book to me."

He slid down the bed and lay down on his side facing me. He held the book to his chest and cupped my jaw. He didn't pry, he didn't push for answers. He just stared at me.

"She would read a few pages to me every night," I told him. "It was my favorite book."

"Oh, Brent," he whispered.

There was only concern in his eyes, no pity, no doubt. Maybe that was why I told him. Maybe there were other reasons. Maybe some part of me wanted him to know, needed him to know.

Whatever it was, I didn't question it. I just talked.

"I had the best childhood. I was just your average kid, did okay at school, played sports. Got to high school and my parents had really high expectations: you know, football, grades, college…" I sighed. "You know, I always thought a parent's love was supposed to be unconditional. I always thought they'd love and support me no matter what… But when I was fifteen, I told them I was gay," I finished quietly. "Well, I'd been wrong about love being unconditional."

Logan rubbed his thumb along my face. He still didn't speak. He just listened.

"Anyway, I found out there were some things my parents wouldn't accept. Or forgive. My mother was horrified, but I think she was more worried about what her church group would think and what gossip she'd be subject to."

"And your dad?"

I exhaled loudly. "Well, he threatened to beat it out of me, and that's when my grandma stepped in, Dad's very own mother." Logan looked mortified, so I gave him a small smile. "I can't even remember why she was at our house, but she was there and witnessed the whole thing. She stood between me and my father and told me to go upstairs and pack my bags."

Logan blinked, wide-eyed, and was paler than usual.

"I heard them from upstairs," I went on to say. "Dad was yelling about religion and God, and my grandma yelled back, telling him the only one God would be ashamed of was him. I came back downstairs with my school bag and a bag of clothes, and we left. I haven't seen them or spoken to them since."

Logan shook his head and whispered, "Oh my God."

"Grandma went back a few days later to get more of my stuff, but that was it. I don't know what was said that day, but Grandma never spoke to them again." I looked at Logan, and his eyes were glistening. I covered his hand on my face with my own and brought it down between us. His fingers squeezed mine. "That's my biggest regret, that Grandma died without making peace with her own son."

Logan shook his head. "Oh, baby."

I looked back at *Treasure Island*, which Logan now clutched to his chest. "I don't have many fond memories of my mother, but this book is one of them."

Then tears spilled down to his temple.

I closed my eyes and whispered, "Please don't cry."

He didn't say anything. But with a strength that surprised me, he pulled me into his arms so my face was buried into his neck, wrapped his arms around me, and he just held me. So fucking tight.

I felt relieved that I'd told him about my parents. It was freeing. But it was something more than that. It was opening myself up to him. I'd just told him something I'd only told a few people, and I knew what it meant. I was letting him in. It was both frightening and exhilarating.

After a long while, I broke the silence. "Logan?"

He stroked my hair. "Yes?"

"Would you keep reading to me?"

He kissed the top of my head, rolled onto his back, and keeping my head on his chest and his free arm around my shoulder, he started on chapter two.

CHAPTER NINE

I WAS LOST in the story, lost in Logan's voice, and the feeling of being wanted and accepted. I couldn't ever remember feeling so at peace until he stopped reading, kissed the top of my head, and whispered, "Are you asleep?"

I answered him just as quietly, "No. Why?"

"You're so quiet. You're never this quiet."

I lifted my head off his chest, looked at him, and smiled. "I could listen to you read for hours."

He smiled warmly and pulled my face in so he could kiss me. And he kept on kissing me, wider, deeper, slower, and holding me closer, tighter. Then he murmured, hot in my ear, "How about we try making it four?"

Four.

Four? Oh, four. I'd forgotten my little quest to see how many times I could make him come in one day.

We were still only in our underwear, so it didn't take much to undress. I crawled off the bed and stood next to it, dragged him by his legs so his ass was at the edge, and pulled off his boxer briefs in one swift movement. I quickly grabbed supplies from his bedside drawer, and when I looked back at him, the sight made my breath catch in my throat.

This beautiful man, his long, pale legs splayed open for me, his cock lying long and heavy on his stomach, looked at me with darkened eyes and nodded. I lifted his legs, pushing them up towards his chest, exposing his ass to me.

I swiped my tongue down the length of his cock, over his balls, and across his hole. And he moaned.

Then I licked him, pressing the tip of my tongue inside him. And he groaned.

Then I spread lube on my fingers and inched them inside him, stretching him, prepping him. And he fisted the sheets at his side and begged me.

He begged me.

I quickly rolled a condom on and edged my aching cock inside his tight, hot ass. I gripped his hips and sank, slowly, oh-so-fucking slowly inside him. He lifted his legs higher, locking his feet behind me, giving me all of him.

And I took it.

Over and over, as slow as my body would allow, I pressed into him, thrusting, thrusting. I leaned down to kiss him, needing his mouth on mine. He arched into me, and I pushed in impossibly deeper.

Logan slipped his arms around my neck, and he held me to him, squeezing me with his legs, with his ass. His mouth and tongue were fused to mine, and I slipped my arms under his shoulders.

All I could do was roll my hips, flexing into him. My balls were on his ass as my body bent over his. It was slow. It was sweet. It was emotion and need. It was beautiful.

Then he started to shake underneath me as his legs rose higher, tighter, and as I kissed down his jaw and neck, I felt his cock throb between us. Wedged between our bodies, but otherwise untouched, his cock erupted. He dug his fingers into me and threw his head back, and with a silent scream, he came.

Once his body collapsed under me, his legs spread out, releasing his hold on me. So, standing up straight, I gripped his hips and impaled his pliable body, over and over, long, slow, and deep until I surged inside him.

An exquisite fire ran up my legs and down my spine as my orgasm obliterated every cell in my body. I came so hard, so deep inside him, emptying into the condom, again and again.

I don't remember getting up on the bed. I don't remember much of anything, but we dozed for a while before taking a shower. We ordered dinner, sprawled out on the couch, and watched some more *Doctor Who*.

———

IT WAS after eight on Sunday morning, and Logan dropped me off at home in his energy-efficient car so I could get my gas-guzzling truck. I'd need my tools and gear so I could take a look at Beth's storage room electrical problem.

After a quick shower, I told Tim I'd be home after lunch and suggested we do something. I felt bad for not being around much, but he said he understood. He didn't mind. In fact, he found it all very amusing.

I flipped him the bird. He told me he'd line the boys up for a few games of pool, and I told him that sounded great. As much as I enjoyed my time with Logan, I did miss spending time with Tim and even with the others. But then he teased me for sucking up to the sister by fixing shit. I sighed dramatically. "And there I was thinking I missed my housemate."

He laughed, tried to put me in a headlock, and all but pushed me out of the door. "Say hello to the in-laws for me," he crowed.

I flipped him the bird again, and he laughed louder. I smiled as I climbed into my truck, looking forward to this afternoon with the guys.

I followed Logan's directions and found a quaint little storefront with brown brickwork and gold writing on the large glass window. It was in a row of shops—a bakery, a coffee shop, a newspaper stand, and Beth's second-hand bookstore.

I opened the door, making the bell chime, and walked in. There were stacks filled with books under different categories, seemingly placed in some kind of order, and a service counter to the side. It smelled like old paper. I could see why Logan loved it. He'd be in bookworm heaven.

Logan walked out and stopped to smile when he saw me. "Hey."

"Hey," I replied.

"I got you coffee," he told me, walking to the counter where there were two to-go cups.

I smiled at his thoughtfulness. "Thank you."

I took the cup and was looking around the small store when my eyes caught the corner display. "Are those vintage comic books?" I asked, probably a little too excitedly. "Man, I used to love those."

Logan grinned at me and nodded. "Me too." He told me he'd collected them as a kid, just for fun, though, nothing serious, he stressed. "Not like the customers we get. They go berserk over them." I laughed, and he shook his head at me. "If you think I'm a nerd, you should see these guys."

I gasped. "You're an adorable nerd," I said, and with smiling lips, I kissed him. He blushed, a deep scarlet tinting his cheeks and down his neck. Whether he blushed because I called him adorable or because I'd just kissed him in public, I wasn't sure. But it looked sexy as hell on him.

I finished my coffee and suggested I take a look at the back storage room before too many customers came in. I'd warned him earlier that I might need to turn the power off at the mains, so he thought the earlier the better.

I collected my gear from my truck and dumped it in the storage room. Wasting no time, I climbed into the attic to see if I could locate an obvious problem for the light shortage in the storeroom.

The space was like all unused attics—dusty, dirty, and full of spider webs. It was also home to one crispy mouse and chewed-through wires. It'd be an easy fix.

I stuck my head through the access hole and called out to Logan. I showed him the culprit, and he turned his nose up and stifled a strange *eeeeep* sound at the sight of the blackened mouse. He held out the wastebasket for me to drop it into and shuddered from head to foot when it fell into the trash. I chuckled at him and he glared at me. "You'll be washing your hands before you touch me again, mister."

I grinned down at him, and he rolled his eyes, then quickly changed the subject. "So what do you need?"

I already had my flashlight, so I asked him to hand up the reel of cable and my needle-nose pliers and asked him to turn the power off.

He looked at me nervously. "Will you be okay?"

I smiled at him through the hole in the ceiling, and I didn't even roll my eyes. "Yes, I'll be fine."

"How will you know when the power's off?"

I stifled a laugh. "Um, because it will be dark."

He glared at me through the hole, put his hands on his hips, and raised one eyebrow. "Right then, smartass."

I laughed, and he turned on his heel and disappeared from my view. But I heard him mumbling as he walked off. "I can hear you through the ceiling," I called out.

"Good," he shot back from what sounded like the front room. "Then I won't have to ask if you're okay if I do this?" he said, just as he flicked the main power.

I smiled, even though he couldn't see me. "Good," I replied in the dark. "Then I won't have to tell you I'm fine."

I flipped on my flashlight and got started replacing the damaged wires. A few minutes later, I heard the bell on the front door indicating a customer. Then a female, English-accented voice said, "Logan? Why are the lights out?"

"Well, dear sister," he answered, letting me know who he was talking to, "the lights are out so the electrician fixing the lighting problem doesn't end up like the mouse who ate the wires."

"A mouse chewed through the wiring?" Beth asked.

"Yes, it got electrocuted," Logan replied. "Ugh. It was disgusting."

I smiled to myself.

"Is there a lot of damage?" Beth asked, alarmed. "And just how much is a Sunday emergency call going to cost me?"

"He's already paid me," I called out.

There was silence for a long moment until Logan explained, "He can hear through the ceiling, apparently."

"Oh," Beth said. Then she whisper-shouted, "God, Logan, you could have told me."

I chuckled. They sounded alike—their English accents matched.

"I'm almost done," I told them. And not a moment later, I asked Logan to turn the power back on. "Okay, flick the switch in the storage room."

And presto! There was light.

I collected my gear and stepped down the ladder to face a waiting Logan and his sister, Beth. She was tall and slim with long brown hair. They looked alike, even though she didn't wear glasses.

I brushed a spider web from my shoulder and dusted off my hands before extending one out to introduce myself to Logan's sister.

Logan spoke first. "Beth, this is Brent Kelly. Brent, this is my sister, Beth."

We shook hands and I gave her my best smile. "Hi. Nice to finally meet you. Logan talks about you all the time."

And I could see the moment in her eyes when the penny dropped. "You're Brent?"

I nodded. "Sure am."

Logan cleared his throat. "Beth, Brent's an electrician, and he offered to take a look at the problem."

She looked me up and down. "Yes, I can see that. Thank you," she said rather curtly. Her British accent had more bite than Logan's.

I realized then, though I had no clue why, but Logan's sister didn't like me.

The bell at the door rang, signaling a customer. Logan looked at me, then at his sister and reluctantly left us alone to greet whoever had just walked into the store. I started to pack up my gear.

"He thinks very highly of you," Beth said somewhat dismissively, as though to her the idea made no sense.

I smiled regardless. "I happen to think very highly of him too."

"How did you meet?" she asked, point blank.

I sighed, wondering what her angle was. "I took a

shoebox full of receipts and records into my new accountant."

She nodded like she finally understood. "So after he's got you the best tax deal possible, you'll just dump him?"

"What?" I stared at her disbelievingly. I shook my head. "No…"

I couldn't believe this woman. She didn't know me—at all. I'd just fixed her lighting problem in her store—for free —and yet she proceeded to judge me for an asshole.

She gave a loud sigh, as though her own rudeness bothered her. "Look," she started, "you seem like a nice guy, but forgive me for being protective of him. I've always had to look out for him since he was little from people like—" She stopped short.

"From people like me?" I finished for her. "You don't even know me."

Beth looked over her shoulder, ensuring Logan was out of earshot. "Logan's sweet, but he gets taken advantage of." Then she finished quietly with, "I can tell he's taken with you. I just don't want to see him hurt."

"Neither do I," I told her truthfully. "But you should give him more credit. And for what it's worth, I'm rather taken with him too."

Beth stared at me. I think she was trying to gauge the sincerity of my words, or maybe they'd surprised her. Logan walked hesitantly into the storage room. He could obviously feel the tension in the room because he glanced between us. "Everything okay?"

I gave him a smile. "Sure." I picked up my tools. "But I have to get going. I told Tim we'd hang out this afternoon."

He shot his sister a warning glance, then looked at me. "Okay," he said with a tight smile. "Tell him I said hello. And thank you so much for fixing the lights. I'm sure

Beth's very grateful." He gave his sister a pointed stare, prompting her to reply.

"Oh, yes, I am. Thank you," she said. "Really, thank you. And I'm sorry about before. I'm sure you can understand."

And the shitty thing was, I did understand. Logan himself had told me he'd had a rough time at school and college, and that must have been hard for his sister to witness. I gave her a nod, then I picked up the reel of cable and walked over to Logan. "It really was no bother at all," I told him. Seeing the store was empty of customers, save Beth standing behind us, I leaned in and kissed his cheek. His eyes darted to his sister, and a deep blush covered his pale cheeks. I smiled. "Call me tonight?"

He nodded, and I left without even looking to see the expression on Beth's face. But as I walked out of the front door and before it could close behind me, I heard Logan snap at his sister. "What the hell did you say to him?"

———

I WAS on my second beer and losing disgracefully at pool when Tim eyed me cautiously. "Wassup, Brent? I take it meeting the sister didn't go too well. You've been a moody pain in the ass since you got home."

I sighed. He had the tact of a wrecking ball. "No, it didn't go too well."

"Why not?"

I shrugged. "She doesn't like me."

Tim frowned as though the concept was ludicrous. "What the hell's her problem?"

I snorted. "I'm not good enough."

"You're what?"

I shrugged again. "She thinks I'm not good enough," I

repeated. "Well, that's what she implied. That I'm only out to hurt him because *someone like me* couldn't possibly like *someone like him.*"

"That's bullshit."

I looked at Tim, knowing he'd answer me honestly. "Are we that different?"

Tim put his beer down. "You know what? Who gives a fuck what anyone else thinks? What anyone else thinks doesn't matter. As long as you're both happy, it's no one else's business." Then he grinned at me. "And I can see how much you like him."

I nodded and gave a bit of a smile. I'd avoided any kind of permanent relationship, any kind of emotional attachment, refusing to see anyone twice for more than a fuck. But Logan was different. I knew it in my bones. I looked at Tim and said, "I told him about my parents."

Tim blinked. Only he would understand the significance of me telling Logan about my family. "Well, shit…"

I nodded and smiled. "Yeah, I know."

Just then two hands slapped down on my shoulders from behind me. "Look, the prodigal son has returned."

Marty. I turned to face him. "Hey," I said. "How's it going?"

"Good, good," he replied. "Saul's just getting drinks. Who's winning at pool?"

"I am on fire!" Tim crowed, and the usual jokes, teasing, and general not-overly-intelligent conversations between us began.

We had a few more games of pool and a few more beers and basically spent the afternoon laughing. Until Marty asked the loaded question. "So," he drawled out, "when do we meet him?"

"Who?"

He rolled his eyes. "The new man. The guy who's kept

your company for the last three weekends in a row. That we know nothing about."

"Maybe he's imaginary," Saul joked.

"Nah," Tim chimed in. "I've met him."

"You have?" Marty asked, surprised. "What's he like?"

Tim grinned. "He's a nice guy. He's smart, funny, British. You know," Tim said with a laugh. "If I was gay…"

I rolled my eyes and pushed his shoulder. "Shut the fuck up." He laughed, and the other two just smiled and waited for me to tell them something. I smiled nervously, surprised that Tim hadn't told them *something* before now, but obviously he hadn't. I took a deep breath. "His name is Logan. And I'm not sure he's ready to meet you guys."

"Oh, why not?" Marty asked, half joking, half not. "We don't bite. Much." Then he looked at me, somewhat seriously, and said, "Nah, man, that's great. I'm happy for ya."

I nodded at his ability to lie. He wasn't happy at all. "Thanks."

"So," Marty added, "he must be good in bed to keep you interested."

I considered telling him to fuck off, then I considered bragging and telling him he was the best I'd ever had, but all I did was sigh instead. "It's more than that."

"Holy shit," Saul mumbled. He looked in total disbelief at Tim, who grinned and nodded.

Tim held his beer up and turned to face a room of complete strangers. "And it's official!" Tim announced loudly to the entire bar. "Brent Kelly is off the market."

I glared at him, completely embarrassed. "Yeah, thanks, asswipe."

I looked at Marty and Saul. Marty's eyes were wide. "Is he your *boyfriend*?"

I shrugged a shoulder. "Yeah, I guess he is." I smiled at them. "He's different than anyone else I've met. He's quiet and smart. He's got the sexiest accent." God, I was gushing like a school kid.

Saul grinned at me while Marty looked a little… well, peeved.

I'd told him before I wasn't interested in him like that, but he just didn't seem to get it. I clinked my beer bottle to his, trying to lighten the mood and wanting to show him we were still good. "Come on, set the balls up," I said, nodding toward the pool table. "You and me."

He took a pull of his beer and nodded. And the four of us played pool for a while, had a few more beers, and talked utter crap. By the time we left, Marty seemed okay with me, thankfully. I wanted my friends to like Logan. I wanted them to get along.

So when they asked me to bring Logan along for drinks on Friday night, I told them I'd ask.

CHAPTER TEN

I'D HAD a few beers playing pool and was appropriately buzzed and was lying on my bed when Logan phoned that night, like he said he would. He apologized again and again for the way Beth had behaved. He explained how her protectiveness comes off as bitchiness and she really didn't mean any harm.

I told him it was fine. Even as much as her words had stung, she did have his best interests at heart. And in a way, I was glad someone was looking out for him.

He apologized *again*. I told him it was fine, *again*, and laughed. "Logan, really, it's all good."

"You don't think ill of me because of what she said?"

I answered directly, adamantly, "No. Never." Then I changed the subject. "So when can I see you again?"

"Tomorrow afternoon," he said. "We're going computer shopping."

"Oh," I laughed. "That laptop thing again?"

I swear I could hear him roll his eyes. "Yes, Brent."

I laughed again. "Will you come back to my place and help me set it up?"

"Of course."

"Will you stay the night?" I asked. "Ple-e-e-ase?"

He laughed. "Just how many beers did you have?"

I chuckled again. "Only about five or so."

He sighed. "Will you whine about setting up your accounts?"

"No," I lied.

"Will you pay attention while I explain everything?"

"Yes," I lied again.

"You're a terrible liar."

I laughed again. "Will you stay?"

"Yes."

———

I WAS SUPPOSED to meet Logan at the electronics store and was running too late to go home and change. So I turned up in my work boots and dirty work clothes. I brushed as much dust and as many cobwebs off me as I could before I went in, but I was still pretty dirty.

I walked in, grinned at the salespeople, and scanned the large floor. The store was busy enough with customers and staff everywhere and all types of technological stuff I'd never seen before as well as the accessories to go with it.

Then I saw him.

Standing across the floor from me, facing the wall lined with laptops, he wore dark gray pants, his black vest, and his TARDIS blue shirt. I grinned. And my cock twitched.

I made my way over to him, and just a few feet short, a salesgirl stopped me. She stood between Logan and me. "Hello," she said breathily. She very deliberately raked her gaze from my boots to my face. "How can I help you?" I think she was trying to be seductive. I almost laughed.

"Um," I hedged, "you can't help me. Only he can." I

gave a pointed nod to the man behind her, who was smiling at me. I stepped around her and stood right next to Logan. "Hey," I said softly. "Sorry I'm late and dirty. I didn't have time to get changed."

Compared to him, I was a mess, but he smiled beautifully. Fuck, I wanted to kiss him. He looked me over and reached up to pull a tuft of spider web from my hair. I took it from him, and he looked down at my hand. And gasped.

"Bloody hell," he whispered. His accent seemed more pronounced. He took my hand in both of his. "What happened?"

I looked at my bloodied knuckles and shrugged. "Oh, I was under a floor and had my hand jammed against a joist, pulling on cables, and I kept banging my hand."

He looked alarmed. "Does it hurt?"

"Nope." I shook my head. "Just one of the disadvantages of having big hands."

Logan smirked and whispered, "Believe me, there are *no* disadvantages to you having big hands."

The salesgirl behind us cleared her throat, and we both jumped, startled. I'd forgotten all about her. She looked at us, all smiles and twinkling eyes. "Can I help you guys with anything? To do with computers?"

I laughed and stood aside. "Um, Logan?"

"This is your laptop," he said with a smile. "You need to have some input."

I grinned at him. "I really like that blue shirt on you."

The salesgirl giggled, and Logan rolled his eyes, ignoring me completely. Then he launched into some spiel on deals for laptops, and I just stopped listening after he started on about processors and compatibility. But it was awesome to watch. It was soon pretty obvious that he knew more about all things technological than the salesgirl, and it really didn't take us very long. We were back at my place less than an hour later.

And for the next hour or so, we set everything up, and Logan showed me the basics. He started with spreadsheets, saying there was no point in getting me used to complicated software. I agreed wholeheartedly, even though I thought spreadsheets looked complicated enough.

He set up monthly sheets with expenses and taxes that somehow calculated formulas to total everything and promised me all I had to do was enter amounts.

By the second hour, I was hungry and horny, and having Logan so damn close to me was too big a distraction. And far too tempting.

He sat at the table facing the laptop, and I sat, facing him. I leaned in, getting closer and closer until my nose traced the side of his neck. "You have the most beautiful skin," I murmured, and he moaned quietly.

"Brent," he groaned, "we need to finish this."

I kissed along the side and back of his neck and hummed. "Mmm, the way your hair curls at the back of your neck. The way you smell. Have I mentioned how much I like this shirt on you?"

Logan turned in his chair. His eyes were dark and he licked his lips. And I knew our computer time was done. I stood up, pulled out my wallet, and threw it on the table. "Hey, Tim?" I called out to my housemate, who was watching TV. "There's money for dinner. Order if you want something. We'll be busy for a while."

Taking his hand, I led Logan into my room. "I can't make you come five times in one day, then not at all for two days," I told him very seriously, kissing his lips, jaw, and neck. "That's not right."

I pulled his vest off, unbuttoned his shirt, then undid

his pants. I slid my hand into his briefs and stroked him, hard.

"I need you," I told him. "I really need to be inside you."

He leaned into me, thrusting his hips into my fist, and he moaned. "Oh God, yes. Now, baby. Now."

I turned him around and bent him over the bed. I pulled his pants down over his ass and quickly undid my work pants. With his pants around his thighs and mine still on my hips, I rolled a condom on, slicked my cock, then his ass with lube, prepping him crudely before I pressed the head against his hole. "You sure, baby?"

"Yessss," he groaned, fisting the bed covers and trying to push his ass against me. "Please."

So I pushed inside him. In one swift thrust, I was completely sheathed in him. He moaned like I'd never heard from him before. The sounds that escaped him, oh God, what those sounds did to me. They spurred me on, urged me, begged me to thrust and fuck, to pump him harder, harder, harder.

Anything to hear him moan like that.

And when I leaned over him, pushing every inch of my cock into his tight hole, I rolled my hips, making him groan low and loud. There was something about the urgency, about the pure need—we were still both dressed with our pants around our thighs—and I knew he felt it too. He was raising his hips off the edge of the bed to meet me, moaning and begging.

"Pump yourself," I urged him, unable to take my hands from his hips.

He came after only a few strokes, and when I finally erupted into the condom, he collapsed under me, exhausted, sated, chuckling.

I kissed his shoulder. "Are you okay?"

"Mmm," he hummed. "Better than okay."

I chuckled with him, nipping at his shirt. "It's this TARDIS shirt. It does something to me."

He laughed under me. We eventually got up, showered, and ate some of the pizza Tim had ordered for dinner, only to go back to bed. We didn't do anything sexual, just lay in bed, with him tucked into my arms.

"Hey, babe?" I asked.

He was tracing circles around my nipples with his fingertip. "Yeah?"

"I want you to come with me on Friday night to meet the guys."

His fingers stopped on my chest. "You do?"

I nodded. "Yeah."

He sighed, and after a long beat of silence, he said, "Okay."

———

LOGAN CAME OVER AGAIN on Tuesday night to help me sort my accounts on my new laptop. He spent time talking and laughing with Tim while I did all the typing, but he didn't stay the night. And on Wednesday and Thursday, I only spoke to him on the phone.

By Friday night, I was itching to see him. And he was nervous as hell about meeting my friends. Even though he said he wasn't, I could tell he was. He spent ten minutes ranting to me over the phone about what the hell to wear. I laughed, which didn't help the situation, and in the end, I told him to just be himself. "Just come to the bar straight from work," I suggested, and he sighed.

I told him he didn't have to come if he didn't want to, but he swore he'd be there. He'd meet me there around six.

Tim and I got there around five-thirty, and the after-work crowd was filing in. The place was kind of a sports bar with screens showing various sports channels and a good mix of people—gay and straight, students and professionals.

We grabbed a table, and Marty and Saul arrived soon after. They were surprised to see me there. Marty said, "Oh, no boyfriend tonight?"

I smiled at him. "He's meeting us here."

Marty's mouth fell open, but he recovered quickly with, "That's good. I want to meet the man who snagged you."

I put down my beer. "Look," I huffed, "be nice to him, Marty, or fuck off and go home."

He blinked, shocked at my tone. "Jeez, Brent. So touchy."

Tim intervened, talking about work and whatever else, while I kept my eye on the door. The place was getting full with its usual Friday night crowd, and at about ten to six, I spotted him.

I grinned. "There he is," I mumbled more to myself than anyone else and made my way over to get him. He was wearing his dark gray pants and a black jacket. His dark hair and black-rimmed glasses made his skin look even paler and his lips even pinker than usual. Fuck, he was gorgeous.

"Hey," I said, still smiling. I leaned in and kissed him quickly.

His gaze darted around us and he blushed. "Hey."

I took his hand. "Come on, they're over here," I said, leading our way through the crowd. And when we got to the table, Tim grinned through his hellos and offered to get him a drink. Marty and Saul just stared.

"Logan," I said, making introductions, "this is Saul."

They exchanged polite hellos, and with a pointed stare, I said, "And this is Marty."

Marty was polite enough. Too polite for my liking, as though he found Logan amusing. And not in a good way. But he wasn't down-and-out rude, so I just made sure there was a safe distance between them.

We spent most of the night just chatting, and after a few drinks, Logan seemed to relax. He was laughing with Tim and Saul over something, which was why I didn't think twice about leaving the table to take a piss. I simply gave Logan's hand a squeeze and told him I'd only be a minute.

When I walked out of the restroom, I saw Tim at the bar, Saul chatting with an old school friend, which left Logan alone with Marty. Then I saw the expression on his face. It was like slow motion, with no sound. I could see the hurt on Logan's face as he stood, grabbing his jacket off the back of his chair. I could see Tim back at the table, trying to talk to Logan, then turning and pointing his finger and cussing at Marty.

I made my way over to them through the crowd, probably knocking a few people too roughly, only to hear Logan say he was leaving.

I slid my hand around his waist, about to ask him what had been said, but he stepped away from me.

"I thought you were different," he said to the ground. As he turned to leave, even over the noise of the bar, I heard him just fine. "God, I should have known better."

CHAPTER ELEVEN

"LOGAN, WAIT!" I cried, grabbing his arm. "Don't go."

He shucked off my hand, and ignoring me, he wove his way through the crowd toward the exit. I turned back to Marty and yelled, "What the hell did you say to him?"

Marty stood up from his chair. "What someone should have said to him weeks ago."

Tim put his hand on my shoulder. I thought it was to calm me down, but it wasn't. Tim looked at me then and said, "Marty told Logan you were only fucking him to get tax benefits."

I gripped the table so I didn't close my fist and punch him. I wanted to. Fuck, I wanted to, but I wanted to go after Logan even more. I turned to leave and had taken only two steps when Marty called out, "He was a fucking queen, anyway."

And that did me in. I turned on my heel and cleared the table between us. I swung at the son of a fucking bitch Marty, connecting my fist with his face, sending him flying backwards.

I tried to hit him again, but there were too many hands

on me, holding me back, restraining me. Someone helped Marty to his feet. He held his hand to his bloodied nose and looked at me with shock and apology in his eyes, but it wasn't enough. I swung at him again, then two security guys dragged me out of the door, throwing me into the street.

Tim followed me out without any help from security, and grabbed me, stopping me from trying to get back inside. "Forget Marty," he told me. "Logan left."

I looked around the darkened street. "Is he still here?" I looked back to the two men who stood at the door. "Was there a guy out here? Tall, glasses… Did you see where he went?"

One of them took pity on me. "Taxi. That way." He nodded up the street.

My first instinct was to go to Logan's house and knock on his door until he agreed to see me. But then I stopped.

He wouldn't want to see me. Why would he? He thought I'd used him. He thought I was like all the other assholes who teased him, bullied him. *I thought you were different,* was what he'd said. That he should've known better.

I'd be the last person he'd want to see.

"Come on," Tim said, leading me towards the waiting cab. "We'll go find him."

Trying not to cry, I climbed into the taxi and shook my head. "I'll just go home," I mumbled and told the cabbie the address.

Tim slid in beside me, slammed the door, and stared at me. "What? You're just gonna give up?"

Unable to look at him, I stared out of the cab window. "He won't want to see me."

The rest of the cab ride was quiet. Well, Tim tried to talk, and I told him to shut the fuck up. And when we got home, I walked into the kitchen and grabbed a beer from the fridge and some ice from the freezer. My knuckles were cut and throbbing.

Tim followed me and threw his keys on the kitchen counter. "Fucking hell, Brent," he huffed at me. "You finally have someone in your life worth holding onto, and you're just gonna let an asshole like Marty fuck it up for you?"

"What else am I supposed to do?" I yelled at him, my anger misdirected. "He's too good for me. It's always been there, hanging over us, the differences between us. Even his sister saw it!"

Tim scoffed. "His sister was being a bitch."

"He's better than me. He deserves someone better than me. Someone smarter, someone who knows what the fuck he's talking about when he's trying to explain statistical finance."

Tim snorted and shook his head. "He's not any better than you. You're just different, but neither one is better or not better than the other. Brent, you're a good guy, one of the best guys I know. And any guy, regardless of how smart he is or what he does for a living, would be lucky to have you."

I took the ice pack off my hand and put it on my forehead. I was getting a headache, and maybe the cold would stem the tears that kept threatening to fall.

Suddenly there was a knock at the door. I took the ice pack off my forehead and looked at Tim. "If that's Marty, I'll fucking kill him."

I stood in the kitchen doorway, looking to see who it was Tim let inside. But it wasn't Marty.

It was Logan.

The first thing I noticed was that he'd been crying, and

it twisted my gut. The second thing I noticed was he was holding some papers.

He swallowed hard. "This is your tax return." He walked over to the dining table and pulled out a pen. "If you sign it now, then you'll be free of any obligation to see me."

I shook my head. But the words wouldn't come. My eyes stung and my chest hurt. But I somehow walked over to him and picked up the pen. "It wasn't like that," I said softly. "Please listen—"

"You don't have to explain." He shook his head and lifted his chin. "In fact, I'd rather you didn't."

"But what Marty said wasn't true."

"Brent, please don't make this any more difficult."

And I understood then. It was too late. He wanted nothing to do with me. It shouldn't have surprised me, but the hollow ache in my chest burned, making my eyes fill with water.

I sucked back a breath and willed myself not to cry. Fuck, I hadn't cried in years. I shook my head and signed the paper. And I wasn't just signing my stupid fucking tax return. I was signing us done. That was it. It was over.

I looked at him, and I know the tears in my eyes surprised him, but still, he said nothing. He was so composed, so together. And I was fucking falling apart.

"Please don't," I started to say, but he picked up the papers and took a step back.

I wanted to tell him to stay. I wanted to tell him to stop. But as he turned and walked to the front door, I couldn't make a sound.

"Logan, wait!"

Those were the words I wanted to say, but it was Tim who said them. I looked at him, my best friend, as he walked over to us. "Logan, please," he started. "What

Marty said isn't true. So if you're gonna leave, if you're gonna end things with Brent, then at least do it over something he did, not some bullshit story Marty made up."

Logan looked at Tim and swallowed hard but said nothing. He just waited for Tim to finish.

And I... I just stood there.

Tim looked at me, then back at Logan and told him, "Brent doesn't give a shit about taxes or how much refund he'll get back. He never has. Marty's just a jealous asshole who'd say anything to get his hands on Brent, and when he saw how Brent looked at you, he knew he didn't stand a chance."

I stared at Tim. He was talking about me like I wasn't even there. He was talking for me, saying all the shit I could never say.

Tim looked back at me and sighed, then turned to face Logan. "If you had any idea what Brent was like before he met you, you'd understand. You'd see how different he is now."

Logan finally looked at me then. And I thought for one second I saw a flicker of something in his eyes, but then he shook his head. "I can't..." And he turned to leave.

"Logan, please." This time the words were mine. They were barely a whisper, but he heard them, and he stopped. When he looked at me, I tried to tell him, I tried to say the words that would make him stay. "I... I, um, I..."

Logan shook his head and turned back toward the door. He must have thought my inability to speak meant I had nothing to say. But I had so much to say. There was so much to say, I just couldn't say the words out loud.

"Logan, Brent's in love with you."

Logan and I both turned to Tim, both of us gaping, and Tim nodded. He stared at Logan and continued, "He just can't tell you. His fucked-up parents did a real number on him. He has a hard time with saying shit out loud, but it doesn't mean it's not true."

They both looked at me then, just in time to see the first of my tears fall. I scrubbed at my face, only to wince at the pain in my knuckles.

"Oh, Brent," Tim said softly with sadness in his eyes. "I'm sorry, buddy. But it's true."

I nodded and wiped my cheeks again. "I know," I croaked out. And for some reason, I didn't want to stand up anymore. I was suddenly fucking exhausted. I needed to sit down. I fell onto the sofa, my head fell back, and I closed my eyes. "Logan," I said quietly. I took a shaky breath, and even with my eyes closed, more tears fell. "It's okay. You can go if you want. I just want you to know that what Marty said wasn't true."

After a long silence, I heard the quiet click of a door, and I knew Logan had gone. So when someone knelt on the floor in front of me, I slowly opened my eyes, expecting to see Tim.

But it wasn't. It was Logan.

He had tears in his eyes, and he reached out and took my hand. "What happened to your hand?" he asked quietly.

"I punched Marty," I answered flatly. "He was lucky all I broke was his nose."

Logan's long, gentle fingers traced over the bruised and bloodied knuckles. He whispered, "Did you break your hand?"

I opened and closed my hand a few times and answered him just as quietly. "I don't think so."

Logan was silent for a long moment. Then he asked, "Is what Tim said true?"

I nodded. "Yeah, it's hard for me. I can't... I've never had..." I shook my head and my eyes welled with tears again. "It's hard for me to talk about stuff like that… what Tim said."

He spoke, looking to the floor. "Why me?" he asked. "I mean, you could have any guy you wanted. You're athletic with blond hair, blue eyes…" He shook his head and sighed quietly. "You're absolutely gorgeous. It doesn't make sense you'd want a geek like me."

"Logan…" I lifted his chin so he'd look at me. "You have no idea how sexy you are. Your body, your lips, your accent, even your glasses…" I smiled at him, wiping my cheek with the back of my hand. But then I told him seriously, "The way you think, how you see the world… your mind… it's a beautiful thing."

Logan blushed and smiled, then his lips twisted sadly and he sighed again. "I'm sorry I believed him and not you," he said, still whispering. "I just never understood why you'd want me. I've spent my life being the punchline of jokes for guys like you…" He shook his head. "So when Marty told me you'd even bragged about screwing me to screw the IRS, a lifetime of insecurities made me believe him. I'm sorry."

I cupped my hand to his face, and he leaned into it. "Logan, I would never hurt you like that, not ever." I sat forward, leaned my forehead against his, and taking a deep breath to steel my nerves, I told him, "*Everything* Tim said is true."

Logan's lip curled into half a smile. "Which part?"

I chuckled nervously through my tears. God, he was going to make me say it. I opened my mouth to say it, to tell him… but I couldn't. I just… couldn't.

He held his face to mine. I could feel his eyelashes on my cheek, and he whispered, "You love me?"

I gasped, and I tried to answer him with words, but they were stuck in my throat, strangling my heart. I couldn't say them, so I nodded. "When you read that book to me…"

And I could feel him smile into my cheek. His fingers slid into my hair and he pulled my face from his. His eyes were bright and shining, filled with tears, and he nodded. "I love you too."

I huffed out a breath of relief, and before I could even smile, he kissed me. It was a different kiss, a reverent kind of kiss. This man, this beautiful man loved me. And with that overwhelming, heightening, humbling realization, I knew what I wanted. I wanted to give myself to him.

He already had my heart. I wanted him to have my body too.

Breaking the kiss, I stood up and led him to my room. I walked to my bedside table, and when I handed him a condom, he looked at me, confused.

"I want… I want you…" I fumbled with my words, not sure how to ask. "Logan, I need…" I huffed out a sigh, unable to say the words.

Logan looked at the condom in his hand, then looked to me. "You want me… to *top*?"

I sucked back a breath and nodded. "I want that with you."

His eyes were wide and he looked a little scared. "I've never done that," he said quietly.

"Then I'll be your first." He still looked a little hesitant, so I kissed him softly. "Please."

His eyes searched mine, and after a long moment, he nodded. I let him take the lead. I needed him to take charge. I wanted him to take care of me, to possess my body, to use it for his pleasure. I wanted him to claim me.

I needed it.

He undressed me, savoring each reveal of skin with his hands, his lips. I lay face down on my bed, and he kissed my back and neck while his fingers pressed and probed and prepped me. And when he finally knelt between my thighs and leaned over me, I was desperate to have him inside me.

He took his time, and he took my breath away. He was slow, and he was so sure as he inched inside me, filling me, fucking me. I groaned shamelessly, gripping the sheets and gritting my teeth as he pushed all the way in. And when he could go no farther, when his balls were flush against me, he panted and puffed, and asked if I was okay.

"Yes, yes," I grunted, lifting my hips, pushing against him. "Fuck me, please."

And he did. He started to slide inside me, thrusting and groaning. It stung and stretched me, but I liked the burn. I lifted my hips higher, giving him more of me, and he lay over my back with his hips flush on my ass, kissing my shoulder, and his long, rigid cock so far inside me.

God, he was so far inside me. Every fucking inch.

The pressure built in my belly, in my chest. It took me a moment to realize it wasn't an orgasm. It was a different kind of release. And I wanted it, I *needed* it, and as Logan's thrusts became erratic, out of rhythm, I knew he was close.

So was I. I was so close.

And when he bucked and pounded me, he screamed into my neck and pulsed inside me as he came. His long cock surged, spilling into the condom, and it was all I needed. He'd claimed me, taken me, and made me his. And my release filled my chest and warmed my blood. It wasn't a physical release, but an emotional one.

Logan rolled me over, and he was obviously shocked to find more tears. "Did I hurt you?" he asked, alarmed.

"No." I shook my head and smiled through my tears. "No, it was just what I needed," I told him. I leaned up and kissed his lips. "You are just what I needed."

His smile died quickly. "I never made you come."

I kissed him again. "I didn't need to. It was more than that. Next time you will." He looked at me with questioning out-of-focus eyes. I chuckled at him and kissed his eyelids, his nose, his lips. "Logan, now you know I am yours," I told him.

He smiled beautifully and snuggled into my neck. "Yes. Like I am yours."

CHAPTER TWELVE

THREE MONTHS LATER

I KNOCKED on Logan's door and grinned as soon as he opened it. He was on his phone, listening to whoever was on the other end babble on. I kissed him soundly as I walked in, making him grin. "Yes, Beth," he said, rolling his eyes, "that'll be fine. See you soon."

Ah, Beth. Logan's sister. We'd made a civil kind of truce. One that involved Logan telling her I was in his life and she could damn well get over it. Then he'd added that she should apologize for being rude to me and take some damn time to get to know me. "Because he's wonderful," he'd said.

He'd told her I was wonderful. It still made me smile.

So she made an effort, and so did I. She really wasn't too bad, and over the last few months, she'd grown on me. She'd even admitted she liked Logan having someone else to look after him.

I didn't bother correcting her. I didn't bother telling her it was he who looked after me. She was just starting to like me. I didn't want to ruin it.

I'd even met his parents. They lived about an hour

away and were more British than the Queen of England. I'd been so nervous, but it was unfounded. They were lovely and welcoming, very much like their son.

Logan closed his phone and kissed me properly. His soft, pink lips were warm and sweet. "Beth just wanted to know if she should bring anything over."

I smiled. "I told Tim to bring some popcorn and whatever he wanted to drink."

Logan grinned. "Is he still freaking out about tonight?"

I laughed and nodded. "But I told him if you had to sit through a night of ice hockey last Saturday night, he could suck it up for a night of *Doctor Who*."

Logan chuckled. It wasn't the first time we'd had video nights where Tim, Saul, and I had got together with Logan, Beth, and her husband, Michael.

Needless to say, Marty was no longer in our lives. He'd tried to apologize, many times. But I was having none of it. I wanted nothing to do with him.

Last time we'd all met, it had been Tim's choice for entertainment, and he'd demanded that a night game of ice hockey be involved that Saturday. Logan had been horrified but had sat through it with his eyes squinted shut most of the night and had promised next time he'd pay him back with a night of *Doctor Who*.

And that was exactly what we were doing.

Logan started fussing in the kitchen, saying Beth and Michael would arrive in about thirty minutes, and we'd better get organized. I smiled as I watched him busy himself with dishes and snacks, dressed in his tight jeans, black turtleneck sweater, and black-rimmed glasses.

I was in love with this man, this unlikely, totally geeky, fucking beautiful man. I'd been working on my ability, or lack thereof, to speak from the heart, and Logan had played a huge part in that. The man had the patience of a saint.

He also had the amazing ability to both anchor me and set me flying at the same time. He'd said I did the same for him, and I'd told him I didn't see how that was possible. He'd just grinned and shook his head and had told me one day I'd see just what he meant. He'd said he didn't mind how long it took—one year or twenty—he'd be there to show me.

And I didn't doubt him.

I smiled at him. "Hey, babe?"

He looked up from his chopping board. "Yeah."

"I got you something."

"You did?"

I nodded and showed him the small, white paper bag.

"What is it?"

"Open it and find out."

He took the bag, grinning excitedly, and looked inside. His eyes shot to mine, and I smiled at him as he pulled out the gift. It was a keychain with a small, three-dimensional TARDIS hanging off it. And attached to it was a single silver key.

"I found the little TARDIS key ring the other day," I told him. "But I had the key to my place cut this morning."

His eyes went wide and he looked from the key ring in his hand to me. "Brent…"

"I want you to have a key to my place. I asked Tim if he'd mind, and he was surprised you didn't have one already."

Logan shook his head. "Oh…" He sighed. "This is… perfect."

"What? Me? Or the TARDIS key ring?"

Logan smiled and rolled his eyes. "The key ring, of course."

My mouth fell open indignantly, playfully. "Do you only love me for the *Doctor Who* stuff I buy you?" I looked over to the TARDIS cookie jar and the Dalek teapot.

He laughed, took my chin between his forefinger and thumb, and kissed me with smiling lips. "I love you, Brent Kelly."

"Just as well," I told him, trying not to grin. "Because I could take the key ring back to the store and get my five bucks back."

Logan laughed. "I hope you kept the receipt."

I grinned at him then. "Of course."

He chuckled at me and went back to the chopping board.

I watched him for a moment. "Logan?"

"Yes?"

"I love you too."

EPILOGUE

FOUR YEARS LATER

THE SMALL RING box in my coat pocket felt as big and as heavy as a box of nails, and I swore everyone in the crowded convention center looked at me like they knew. It was as though it was some great conspiracy that all *Doctor Who* fans had some wibbly-wobbly, timey-wimey powers and they somehow knew...

Oh, Jesus. Did I actually just use the words wibbly-wobbly, timey-wimey?

I knew it was ridiculous to think everyone knew what my plans were. There was just simply no way they could, but it didn't stop the feeling that I had a massive flashing neon sign above my head that everyone but Logan could see.

I had worried that he might have guessed something was up, but if he did know I was planning something, then he hadn't let on. He was so much better at keeping secrets than me. I was just about to lose my shit in the middle of a *Doctor Who* convention. Of all the fucking places.

I'd thought Logan might clue in when I'd suggested we go. I mean, it wasn't every day that the stars of his favorite

TV shows came to San Antonio. I think he was too excited to be curious. Then even when Beth and Michael wanted to come along, he'd been excited instead of perplexed by their interest. And when Tim had said he was coming, all Logan had been able to do was shrug. Logan had said he just assumed Tim wanted to come to take the piss out of all the Whovians and that he'd get enough joke fodder to last a year…

He didn't seem to think it strange.

He certainly didn't seem to think I was planning to ask him to marry me.

Tim kicked the side of my boot. "Pull yourself together," he whisper-shouted at me. "He's gonna know something's up if you don't take it down a notch or two."

"I'm trying," I whispered back at him. "I'm kinda freakin' out, all right?"

He pulled me to the side, away from the hordes of Whovians crowded around stalls to buy TARDIS merchandise. Logan was looking, of course, though Lord knew he didn't need anything. I'd bought him nearly everything remotely *Doctor Who* related on the internet.

Tim squeezed my arm. "You wanna do this?"

"Of course."

"Do you have any reason to think he might turn you down?"

"Oh, well…" *Fuck.* "Jesus, Tim. I didn't until you mentioned it! Fuck, what if he says no?" I swallowed hard, breathing through the urge to vomit.

Tim smiled at me. "Dude, he's not gonna say no. There is just no way. He's so in-fucking-love with you. And just when I thought he couldn't possibly be any more ridiculously in love with you, you buy him tickets to a freakin' *Doctor Who* convention, and I could see it in his eyes when he went and fell in love with you all over again.

I'm serious, Brent. In the law according to Logan, you created the fucking universe. It really is rather disgusting just how much he adores you."

I snorted out a laugh. Thank God Tim knew just what to say. "He's not gonna say no, is he?"

He shook his head slowly. "Not a chance. He's gonna cry, and he'll probably hit you, then he'll cry some more, but no. He won't say no."

I looked over at Logan, who was still perusing the merchandise tables with Beth and Michael, and smiled. He was wearing light-gray skinny jeans, rolled up at the hems, a fitted black jacket, and a dark gray scarf. His hair was now shaved on one side, longer on top but coiffed up perfectly. His dark-rimmed glasses appeared more accessory than a necessity, even though he was blind without them. He looked like a fucking model. I could stare at him all damn day.

"That's better," Tim said beside me. "Stop freaking out. There's nothing to be freaking out over. It's just Logan. You've lived together, for what, three years?"

"Almost three, yeah."

"You *know* him. You have nothing to panic about."

"You're pretty smart, you know that?" I said to Tim. "I mean, for a dumbass."

He whacked my shoulder just as Logan cut through the crowd on his way over to us. He was carrying something. Oh good. Just what we needed. More *Doctor Who* stuff...

His response was rather short and simple. "If you thought you could bring me here and I wouldn't buy more things, then you were very wrong."

I slid my arm around his waist and kissed the side of his head. "I didn't expect anything less."

"Well, good," he replied, "because there's a whole other section of stalls over there."

"The 'meet the actors' thing is on soon," I reminded him. "And the photo thing."

Logan looked at his watch. "We still have plenty of time." He gave me a smile that usually would have made me melt before he turned and went scouting for more merchandise.

The *photo thing*, as I'd called it, was where I was going to ask him to marry me. People could pay a fee and have their photos taken inside a TARDIS, and I thought it would be the most perfect place…

"It's okay," Beth said, resting her hand on my arm. "I'll hurry him along."

"Yeah, the sooner the better, I think," Tim added. "All this waiting is killing him. He'll be back to thinking Logan's gonna turn him down if we don't make this happen soon."

Beth's eyes softened. "Oh, Brent, love," she said, her British accent sounding thicker. "No, no, no. He won't be turning anything down, I can promise you that."

They were so sure.

And I would be too if I could just get this over and done with. I knew he loved me, I really did. And the logical side of my brain said this was the best idea, ever. But my nerves were playing havoc with me. I took a deep breath, then released it slowly. "I'm so nervous."

"Right," Beth said with a hard nod. "Time to make it happen. I'll have him through those doors over there in two minutes."

Well shit! Two minutes wasn't very long.

Two minutes!

Fuck, there was no way I was going to be ready in two minutes.

Tim laughed. "Oh, Brent, for God's sake," he said, pushing me toward the double doors that led through to the auditorium. There were a thousand people walking in all sorts of directions, most dressed in some kind of *Doctor Who* costume. Then I lost sight of Logan, and Tim was still pushing me in the opposite direction, and I was pretty sure I was about to have a shit-fit.

"Stop panicking," Tim urged me quietly. "He's just there, see?" He nodded over my shoulder, and when I turned, sure enough, Logan was there looking at some stall of striped scarves, bowties, and red fezzes. Beth was soon by his side, dragging him toward us.

I felt relieved as soon as I saw him. It was a sense of calm, a sense of right. I was going to ask him to marry me. I wanted to spend my life with him, and I knew it was absolutely the right thing to do when just the sight of him made my world right itself.

Logan took my hand and looked at me questioningly. "You okay?"

I nodded. "Never better. But I was wondering… I was… Would you like to have your photo taken in the TARDIS now?"

Logan eyed me cautiously, then Tim, then Beth, then back to me. "You sure everything's all right?"

I squeezed his hand. "Absolutely." I looked over to where the line-up was, and still holding his hand, I led the way. There were probably twenty or so people ahead of us in the line, which meant more waiting, but this was happening. I was doing this. Shit, I was really doing this. I had to let go of his hand to wipe my palms on my jeans.

"Are you feeling okay?" Logan asked. "We can sit out if you're not feeling too great."

I tried to shake off my nerves and give him a smile. "I'm great."

He narrowed his eyes at me. I was a terrible liar, and he was too polite to call me on it in front of people.

"Oh, Logan," Beth interrupted. "What was the name of the sixth Doctor?"

Logan answered, and Beth argued, which was ridiculous because he knew every detail of the show, and she'd have had more sense to argue tax laws with him. It was a ploy to distract him and to give me a minute to breathe.

Tim smiled at me. "You look like you could use a beer."

I puffed out a breath. "Man, you have no idea."

Beth and Logan argued about names until the line got smaller and smaller, and finally—finally—we were next.

I snatched up his hand, more for my own sake than his and waited for the nod from the attendant to tell us it was our turn. Logan's irritation at his sister defused when he saw the TARDIS up close, and his grin was spectacular.

"Okay." The staffer waved her hand at us to come over. "Next."

Logan was kind of bouncing on his toes. His excitement was palpable.

The attendant smiled warmly at us, while the photographer fiddled with his camera. "Both of you in the TARDIS together?"

Before Logan could answer, I said, "How about you first? We'll have one of just you, then one of both of us?"

"Oh," he said with half a shrug. He gave me a quick confused look, but thankfully—thankfully—he went along with it.

Now, this could all go spectacularly wrong. And I immediately regretted not lining this up with the attendant beforehand. I was just winging it. Which was a tactic I'd kind of done my whole life, and one I was starting to regret. This really could have used some foresight.

"Okay then," the woman said, all but pushing Logan into the TARDIS. "Close the door and open it on three."

He shut the door, and the woman called, "One." I pulled out the ring box and stepped forward. I heard the photographer take some shots.

"Two," she called, giving me a what-the-hell kind of look.

I knelt down.

"Three."

He opened the door, and I opened the ring box.

Logan was giving his best photogenic smile toward the camera, but then he looked down. Then he saw me. Then he saw what I was holding.

His hands went to his mouth, and a collective gasp went around the auditorium. Everyone was watching. Someone squealed. He still hadn't answered. He still hadn't moved. His hands were still covering his mouth, and his eyes filled with tears.

"Logan," I said, or squeaked. I really wasn't sure at this point. "If I had two hearts, they'd both belong to you. Would you, Logan Willis, have me as your companion through all of space and time?"

You could have heard a pin drop.

Logan stepped out of the TARDIS, tears now flowing down his cheeks, and changed my life forever.

He nodded.

A massive round of applause and cheers went up around the auditorium, and Logan leaned down, took hold of my face, and kissed me. I got to my feet, legs still shaking, and hugged him so damn hard. We were then consumed by Tim, Beth, and Michael in an all-embracing hug of laughter and tears.

————

THERE ARE NOW two photos that sit on our mantelpiece. One is of me kneeling down in front of Logan, his hands to his mouth. The second photo is of me and Logan, being hugged by Tim, Beth, and Michael. Even the woman attendant was in that hug. The convention photographer really captured the moment perfectly.

Oh, and there's a pretty cool blue police telephone box in the background of each.

I'm pretty sure there'll be one in our wedding photos as well. And you know what? That's perfectly fine with me.

The End

The Spencer Cohen Series, Book Two

The Spencer Cohen Series, Book Three

The Spencer Cohen Series, Yanni's Story

Blood & Milk

The Weight Of It All

Perfect Catch

Switched

Imago

Imagines

Red Dirt Heart Imago

On Davis Row

Finders Keepers

Titles in Audio:

Cronin's Key

Cronin's Key II

Cronin's Key III

Red Dirt Heart

Red Dirt Heart 2

Red Dirt Heart 3

The Weight Of It All

Switched

Point of No Return

Free Reads:

Sixty Five Hours

Learning to Feel

His Grandfather's Watch (And The Story of Billy and Hale)

The Twelfth of Never (Blind Faith 3.5)

Twelve Days of Christmas (Sixty Five Hours Christmas)

Best of Both Worlds

Translated Titles:

Fiducia Cieca (Italian translation of Blind Faith)

Attraverso Questi Occhi (Italian translation of Through These Eyes)

Preso alla Sprovvista (Italian translation of Blindside)

Il giorno del Mai (Italian translation of Blind Faith 3.5)

Cuore di Terra Rossa (Italian translation of Red Dirt Heart)

Cuore di Terra Rossa 2 (Italian translation of Red Dirt Heart 2)

Cuore di Terra Rossa 3 (Italian translation of Red Dirt Heart 3)

Cuore di Terra Rossa 4 (Italian translation of Red Dirt Heart 4)

Confiance Aveugle (French translation of Blind Faith)

A travers ces yeux: Confiance Aveugle 2 (French translation of Through These Eyes)

Aveugle: Confiance Aveugle 3 (French translation of Blindside)

À Jamais (French translation of Blind Faith 3.5)

Cronin's Key (French translation)

Cronin's Key II (French translation)

Au Coeur de Sutton Station (French translation of Red Dirt Heart)

Partir ou rester (French translation of Red Dirt Heart 2)

Faire Face (French translation of Red Dirt Heart 3)

Trouver sa Place (French translation of Red Dirt Heart 4)

Rote Erde (German translation of Red Dirt Heart)

Rote Erde 2 (German translation of Red Dirt Heart 2)

www.ingramcontent.com/pod-product-compliance
Lightning Source LLC
Chambersburg PA
CBHW032047180726
48284CB00004B/1224